CLACKAMAS LITERARY REVIEW

2010
Volume XIV
Clackamas Community College
Oregon City, Oregon

CLACKAMAS LITERARY REVIEW

Editor in Chief
Ryan Davis

Associate Editor
Althea Infante

Assistant Editors
Kristina Barrera
G.G. Brininstool
Kate Bumcrot
Ross Burlingame
Erika Higginson
Angela Hughes
Garret Knauss
Laura Miller
Caitlin Murrell
Devon Seale
Amanda Sherette
Troy Spivey
Autumn Stone

Cover Art
Renee Taylor Boeckman

Cover Design
Charis Woodward

The Clackamas Literary Review is published annually at Clackamas Community College. Manuscripts are read from September 1st to January 31st and will not be returned. By submitting your work to CLR, you indicate your consent for us to publish that work in print and online. This issue is $10; issues I-X are $6 if ordered through *CLR;* issues XI-XIII are available through your favorite online bookseller.

Clackamas Literary Review
19600 Molalla Avenue, Oregon City, Oregon 97045.
ISBN: 978-0-9796882-2-5
Printed by Lightning Source.
www.clackamasliteraryreview.org

Contents

Editor in Chief's Note

Creative Nonfiction

Fiction

Poetry

Contributors

Editor in Chief's Note

Publishing *Clackamas Literary Review* is complicated business, to be honest. Here at *CLR*, the process goes a little something like this:

1. Receive thousands of submissions in five months
2. Gain Assistant Editors
3. Read every submission with respect and serious consideration
4. Choose writing to publish
5. Recognize the subjectivity of editing
6. Confirm our belief in the writing we choose
7. Lose Assistant Editors
8. Freak out, mildly
9. Bow to the everyday work of teaching
10. Gain and lose Associate Editor
11. Notice the time passing, quickly
12. Publish *CLR*, finally
13. Thank the featured writers for their patience

The wait is often long, but, in our opinion, well worth it.

Enjoy,
Ryan Davis
Editor in Chief

Yes
Rachel de Baere

When people ask, *Are you a writer?* Say, *Yes.*
When they ask if you've been published, say,
Yes, I am writing my second book, which you are.

Know you have many books in you –
        the book of letters,
        the YA novel,
        the memoir,
        its sequel.

You haven't finished the memoir.
You're waiting for your mother to die.

In fact, you're so busy writing,
you don't have time to make the bed today, can't
fold the laundry, have to leave the crumbs
shouting at no one to clean them up.

You have books to write –
don't forget the poetry manuscript.

Yes, you are a writer. You must
make time to observe trees, their leaves –
how they start out yellow, curled,
then turn chartreuse, minty even.

You must go to the library,
stay there all day, research
how to pluck a chicken, what it means
to break the glass at a Jewish wedding,
remember your hometown's history –
how the flood happened in 1967.

You have to visit places: Your old house –
it seemed so large to you as a child;
the cobbled streets in front of your grandmother's,
in a country you haven't entered since the King died,
and the village you've never been to but dreamed.

When people see you at the café,
tell them you are working on the book,
so they don't ask
to sit down with you.
You'll see them at the book signing.
Say, *Yes*, of course, they'll be invited.

And don't forget to write.

Fragile

In a box marked –
HANDLE WITH CARE –
the champagne glasses will arrive
from the bridal registry. Packed
in shredded brown paper,
inner boxes will hold the last notes
of clinking crystal,
contain future memories,
rimmed in gold –
forget mosquito bites, neglect nausea,
bury bitter words.
In the public toast, there will be no refuge for her,
just applause, cheers and the voice
of the father who begins the song:
For she's a jolly good fella. The daughter
will cringe in his spill,
cringe at how he is always the first
to propose a toast, needs his glass
to be refilled, again, and again.
Bottled bubbles of champagne will escape
the fruit of their explosive vine.
The daughter will try to bob above it all,
want to appreciate his intent,
revert to wishing the moment
had never happened.

Wild Joy
Darlene Pagán

Under the slide, a boy beats a shoe
against his head to make the little ones laugh
their bubble laughs. Children circle them
hopping, jumping, darting, diving,
all but one who lopes,
his right arm and leg aimed
in another direction
from his left.
He clings to rails, treds steps like
hot coals, but laughs the same bubble laugh
as he throws his head back with
the same devoted sun worship.
The other children thrust their faces
into his before running off and
he growls after them,
one eye shut like a pirate.

On the sidelines with mothers nursing infants
and coffee, I watch him turn a corner
wearing another child's hat
and what has to be the symptoms
of another child's cerebral palsy. But the lines
of his features sharpen into focus
as he falters then falls
again and again until

I set him upright and let him
go. But he doesn't want to go
anymore, lingering at the bench, arm
extended as he begs, *Play pirate ship,*
Mama. Play pirate ship.

I'd have leapt up for the chase
before the diagnosis but now it looks
like the quick and easy rescue. *Go, play,* I insist.
He curls up my arm like a cat though
I tilt my chin up to avoid
his gaze. He stands on tiptoe even
in the brace. I want to force
his leg down, press the heel back the way
the therapist showed us to
stretch the muscle and make him
stand right if he's going to stand there
at all. The wild joy blooms back
in his face as he starts to purr, as this
same child coaxes this new parent
right back onto the playground.

Infatuation
Jodi Adamson

Among the tilt and whirl of these new emotions,
I bob for caramel apples on the Tunnel of Love
With a stranger.
Who is the stranger though?
This man beside me or
Myself, for feeling the way I do?
Would he join me for a spin around the moon and stars?

Famous

Fame's fleeting fingers
Forging a seduction.
I forgive your adultery.
Fall to my knees,
And beg for you back.

Crayola Caste System
Kelly I. Hitchcock

I remember the parade of Crayola crayons
In the jumbo box of eighty distending
From the skipping arms of Melissa Rich
As I shrank under a Rubbermaid craft table
Holding my sixteen box of Rose Arts
With the invisible "just" preceding the label
In one of my small, just-peach hands.
I watched Melissa with my just-blue eyes,
Her first-day-of-school razzle dazzle rose dress
And wild strawberry patent leather shoes,
Tossing her goldenrod curls, blinking her cerulean eyes
Struggling to secure the colossus
Of Crayola crayons with the built-in sharpener
That separated the two of us.

Skipping Stones

Because it can't take the silence
The river whispers through the virgin grove.

In no way inferior, it makes the crickets
Sound their shrillest cries to overcompensate.
In no way scared, it eases over
The intimidating stones and snaky limbs.
In no way inadequate, it waltzes godlike
Gliding inches from the lips of the bank.
In no way guarded, it bares its soul,
Its will stripped naked to the surrounding forest.
In no way lonely, it walks hand in hand
With the fishes and leaves and broken branches.
In no way unfeeling, it invites the moon to dance
And the dragonflies to make love on its silver skin.
In no way an outsider, it reflects the image
Of all who visit its immaculate shelter.

It is in no way like me—
An inferior, scared, inadequate, guarded, lonely, unfeeling outsider
Our only likeness is our superhuman strength

But maybe today, for just a few hours,
I'll let the river be strong for me,
Because I'm tired of being superhuman.

Walking Alone in the Afterlife
Christopher Howell

There is a lark in the loneliness of summer
which winter knows not. Temperature
plays no part in this discrepancy.

I wake in the warm chill of June.
Though I am surrounded by the populace,
no one is near. The lark hands me my name, melodious

with distance and the strangeness of an actual
listener. So here I am again, clouds
and blue shafts of sun. Six years old

or ninety-six, I am in love with something singular,
winged, forgotten by the snow.

The Theology of Cats

My cat asks to know
what I'm doing with this scratchy stick.
I tell him it is a form of love,
that he, too, will be included, no matter
how the stars align or the sea rises,
beyond all thought of strife or flood.
So he nuzzles the pen and lies down
in the consoling heat of my desk lamp.
It is marvelous to note his purring recumbency
and style
sunk in the moment entirely.
With mild fascination he bats at a pencil stub, stretches,
and closes his yellow eyes.
He does not care who God is
or how long he has to live.
He takes no position on gay marriage, abortion,
or school prayer, but I can tell
he would prefer no war distress his sleep,
which is crowded with sunlight
and unsuspecting birds.
Even if he knew all I have failed to do, every good
thing I have broken, he would sprawl happily
among my scribblings and books
and feel no need at all to forgive me.
Perhaps *he* is God.

Lilacs Bloom in the Vacant Lot
Carol Carpenter

Other eighth-grade boys bring tulips
and daffodils that last
a week on Ms. Williams' desk
without releasing one sweet smell.
If I shut my eyes,
I do not even know
they are there.
Their leaves wilt to brown
and the petals drop.

In the vacant lot, next to
the party store, I pick
lilacs. Purple, pink, lavender,
white stars cluster,
arch in bunch after bunch,
so perfect
they look fake. But fake
reeks of plastic. Even I
can smell that kind of lie.
All the way to school,
my lilacs bloom
perfume in the palm of my hand.

One by one, I arrange my lilacs
in Ms. Williams' cut glass vase.
The woody stems touch bottom
as buds on each bunch pop open.

12

My teacher takes huge gulps
of lilac air as if she cannot
catch her breath.

Ms. Williams picks
a sprig from the vase,
tucks it behind her ear
and gasps at the truth of it all.

What Robins and Starlings Have to Say

I just found a dead robin
on the basement floor of my new house.
No, I did not leave
front doors open. I slammed
every window, twisted every lock
against intruders. I swear I did. No,
I have never owned
a cat or dog. I would never accept
a pet whose teeth could crunch fragile bones,
could force me down on hands and knees
in grief. Do not accuse me
of forgetfulness or negligence.
Do not blame me
for this corpse. No.

How did this robin sneak
past me, sidle through
some invisible crack
in the foundation? How?

I only know
the dead robin on the basement floor
of my new house does not sing.
Such silence speaks of red feathers,
a throat swollen with unshed noise.
Do not warn me of death ahead.
Such tittle-tattle tangles me

in dreams where robins peck
me bald, weave my hair into nests
where baby robins rest and chirp
as if nothing can invade their space.

I will bury
my bundle of brown and red,
in a shoebox under the cherry tree.
Let this be the end. I refuse
to see this as an omen.
Death would only dare
present itself as a blue-black starling,

strut across frozen ground
straight to the front door
scream *caw, caw, caw, caw*
until it got in. Its three-pronged feet
would sink into my white carpet,
present another puzzle I cannot solve.

When the Narrator Speaks

If leaves
curl from aphids thick on blaze roses,

release five hundred ladybugs,
a plague of open mouths, a flurry of red-beetle wings.

When the white moon rises
before the pink sun recoils from the day,

turn toward the moon, a mere sliver tonight,
a curve of promise towing the silver sea.

Do not be angry at the red lips of the forest fire
as they gobble green, spit out ash.

Brush aside dust on long, wet days
until pine seedlings stitch scars and fireweed flowers.

And when the creek vanishes in dry air,
when fish flounder on sand and ghosts rustle the grass,

lie down in the bed where nothing can sleep.
Hear the story of stones, the hoarse tale of leaves.

The Living Room as Time Machine
Shura Young

Shafts of Los Angeles' smoggy sunlight pour through the tints and textures of my handmade patchwork curtains. These remnants of my hippie self spread a sun-infused kaleidoscope of colors across tattered furniture, off-white swirled-plaster walls, and the worn gold and white shag rug in the second floor living room of this 1940ish Spanish stucco triplex. Under the impressionistic glow, I sit in my faded olive green chair that is legless on the rug because when one leg broke I removed them all.

A new lover named Rob is going to take the sunlight out of this room causing the colors to vanish. It will remind me of a scene in the 1960 movie, The Time Machine, *in which a time traveler, moving forward faster and faster into the future, is plunged into darkness as boards are hammered up – clack, clack, clack – over the windows of his now abandoned Victorian house.*

I turn on my favorite Billie Holiday cassette and stretch out my legs. On the 1930s recording, Billie's voice is sweet as the gardenia she wore in her hair: "It cost me a lot, but there's one thing that I've got / It's my man, it's my man."

After we're living together, Rob will no longer allow my choice of music in this room.

It is 1978, and I am still the confident "me" in the increasingly multi-ethnic neighborhood between Culver City and Beverly Hills. On this warm October afternoon, I luxuriate in creative aloneness. Self-expression is my religion practiced through art, sex, writing, and freeform dance. Friends call me a free spirit: never wanting to be married, never wanting children, never wanting to be "tied down."

I will lose this "me." In 2003, I will be told I lost my identity and will search back twenty-three years in hopes of finding it. It is why I must revisit the

17

images of this living room, though I know I will never return to the person I was. Because, that person will be brainwashed by Rob into believing that nothing, no one can be trusted, including myself.

Under my 1970's pacifist rainbow, I am complacent with President Jimmy Carter replacing the upheaval of former President Nixon's Watergate and the Vietnam War, and *Saturday Night Live*'s Dan Ackroyd version of President Carter's gentle drawl replacing Chevy Chase in his role as stumbling President Ford.

Josh, my current partner whom I've lived with for two years, is at his UCLA research job. "More fun than summer camp" I call Josh in a playful moment. Josh calls me the most creative person he knows – I write poetry and paint L. A.'s homeless or the molecules of light through my eyelashes, while Josh experiments with abstract collage.

On my lap is my diary, begun twenty years earlier when I was twelve. Or perhaps this day it's a notebook in which I scribble the contradiction between people outside my family who saw my childhood as happy, versus the reality of my abusive father who virtually isolated my mother, brother, and I in our house.

When Rob enters my world, he will appear to possess all the intelligent, poetic sensibilities of my father while masterfully camouflaging the abusive qualities, and worse. Even when Rob no longer suppresses his abuse, he will muddle my mind by giving me affection and attention that my father could never give.

Memory wanders over the living room walls, revisiting original artwork hung there. My favorite is a photograph of me posed nude taken by Josh who has overlaid my face with colored pencil and carved my curve from waist to hip even curvier - until my fluid, dancing body is almost indecipherable. Lucky Josh, living with his own professional artists' model – an income that allows me time to write and paint while providing a vicarious education listening to art professors teach students as they sketch my nakedness.

I listen to and believe Billie as she croons,

> Cold or wet
> Tired you bet
> All of this I'll soon forget
> With my man.

Rob will insist I quit my full-time modeling, wiping out most of my income. He will achieve this by terrifying me with his rage into remaining quiet and immobile in bed in the morning so that he can sleep late without being disturbed – thus disabling me from morning employment. I will wonder how I succumbed to his demands. Was it trauma from the raised-palm rage of my father? The threat of losing love or hunger from never having it?

In my pre-terror freedom of night, I sit cross-legged on the rug working on a painting of the darkened outdoor scene through an open front window. Avant-garde tones of Paul Chihara's *Shiry'u* ballet glide my paintbrush. I'm stirred into excitement molding shadows and night scenes into a myriad of deep, impressionistic colored strokes beyond the typical, boring black and gray. A small oil-on-canvas emerges of the two-story stucco across the street. A splash of yellow-white explodes over the shadowy adobe tile roof – there is a Santa Ana windswept fire burning on distant Mt. Wilson. My completed "Fire on Mt. Wilson" is hung on the wall.

The outdoors that matters very much to me will no longer matter. Aluminum foil will be taped over the living room windows at Rob's insistence on complete blackness during sleep. He will only allow windows opened by permission, and that very seldom. It will be Rob's paranoia and hate injected into my soul that changes my outside view.

Upon the living room wall, I also see a collage-plus-drawing by my artist friend, Lewis. In it, a young woman in print dress is imprisoned at the hips in a wooden pillory. Lewis' hand-made frame is gray-blue with multi-colored dots over which he's glued dozens of tiny electrodes. I am uncomfortable with his view of women, but Josh appreciates the bizarre lens.

After the living room turns dark with only lamps lighting it day and night, and only formal classical music playing, Lewis will again come knocking on the front door. I will peer fearfully through the peephole and let him in, remaining

19

distant until Lewis gets Rob's unspoken message that visitors are not allowed. I will not recognize that this is the beginning of my adult isolation.

Josh and I invite our extended artist, art model, and art teacher family to celebrate my small book, *Grotesqueries, Poems with Drawings,* self-published under Josh's Noble Beast Press – so-named because Josh says I have the profile of a noble beast. Alcohol flows. I sign purchased books until the two hundred-print run is nearly sold out.

Though Josh and I care about each other, our conflicts over my preference for more shared talk and his for less remind me uncomfortably of my fighting parents.

That Josh and I argue at all will push me into searching for a more compatible and passionate love. A love like Rob seems to offer.

As I sip from a mug of warm jasmine tea, Billie sings,

> He's not much on looks
> He's no hero out of books
> But I love him
> Yes, I love him.

Into my luminous hippiedom comes my mother, visiting from Corvallis, Oregon. She persuades me to invite some of my artist friends to a dinner that I cook. We all perch on living room chairs, saggy bed-couch, and rug around the large, rough pine crate topped with a shellacked found-wood slab that acts as makeshift coffee table and doubles as the party dining table. Most often this "table" is strewn with melted candles in holders, artists' charcoal, small sketchbooks with drawings, and books containing the poetry of local poets we've heard at Beyond Baroque readings – Robert Peters, Bill Mohr, Jim Krusoe, Kate Braverman, Deena Metzger. But this night the crate-table only holds eight mismatched dinner plates filled with my homemade spaghetti and salad.

The crude coffee table and second hand bed-couch will be replaced by Rob's tinny television turned on so that his two-dimensional, often dead friends can enter the room. Christopher Lee, Peter Cushing, Bela Lugosi, Vincent Price, Fred Astaire and Ginger Rogers, Frank Sinatra, Rita Hayworth, Dr. Who, James Herriot, and Mary Tyler Moore will replace my real friends. Rob's distrust of live people will become my distrust.

Around the pseudo-dining table, my artist friends discuss the impending loss of our low-income Medi-Cal health care benefits under incoming President Reagan's regime. Mother, seated on the rug beside me, prefers to be the center of attention and interjects with "Did everyone see my necklace?" The boisterous room is silenced until people politely praise the beads then return to their important talk.

At evening's end, Mother finds just the right words for each friend: "You weren't too abrasive this time, Melanie." "Why do you only give side hugs, Evan? I think you're afraid of front hugs." Privately to me she adds, "Carrie's always so cold."

Josh, our artist friends, their art, and the books of poetry are going to disappear forever from this room. Rob will manipulate me away with subtle or not-so-subtle judgments – "Don't you ever inflict those people on me again" or "I think you know your friends aren't the kind of healthy relationships you should have in your life" – until I end up cut off from people who could have helped me see that Rob's control is identical to that of my father's psychological imprisonment of my mother.

As the front door closes on the last dinner guest, my mother – displaying her lifelong emotional unavailability – slumps on the bed-couch and says, "I don't know why we did that. They're your friends, not mine. Not one of them talked to me the whole evening. I don't think they like me." Which is true. They tolerate her. In private, they call her the Dragon Lady.

Rob will bully my mother out of this room. He will enrage her by trying to get her to see that she is not, has never been, "there" for me. He will call her a pseudo-liberal and tell me she's disrespectful, self-centered, intolerant, and vindictive. His method will be wrong, but his view of her will be right, making his demonizing her sound reasonable. Instead of finding a way to offer support in helping me escape Rob's mind control, my mother will claim she no longer has a daughter and will disconnect from my life for twenty years. I will finally view her as the mother who didn't leave my abusive father, who never showed me this choice.

As my mother bemoans having had the party, a spider dangles down from the sparse green and cream pointy-leafed vines she gave

21

me as starts that wander suspended on nails around the uppermost edging between walls and ceiling. I gaze at the descending spider and, with a bit of panic over my inability to get a word in over her constant chatter, I imagine the spider burrowing into her dyed black curly hair and taking up residence. The spider may be dismayed at her return to Oregon, but I'm not.

My plants, unable to sustain Rob's eternal shade, will be banished to a front porch ledge. I'll give up indoor gardening for twenty-four years. When Rob persecutes me just for opening the front door, I will forego outdoor gardens as well.

Alone again, I sit listening to Erik Satie's *Trois Gymnopedies.* My leg-less chair faces the front door with its six-inch cast iron peephole that has a fleur-de-lis embossed hatch I've secured with duct tape, since the latch is broken. Through bars like slender black braids, I greet my array of knocking friends: Carrie,dancer/performer/artists' model for whom I am set designer and stage manager. The lusty, male art model secretary from UCLA Extension Art Studios who gives me rides to modeling jobs there. The shy art student who shaves all the hair on his body. The Japanese-Hawaiian mailman who woos me with creamy pink Oil of Olay samples. And the new man, Rob, Vietnam War protestor and conscientious objector, expert film historian, English literature and sociology graduate, who talks circles around the best intellectuals in a way I view as superior to the poetic nature and knowledge of my father.

I will dream that the iron peephole opens to a frightening man who breaks down the door to attack me. I will awaken blind to the realization that this violent intruder is the "superior" peace activist who darkens the living room, stifles my movement in bed, and whips the kitchen and bedroom with unpredictable rages.

When Rob enters my living room, he fills it with intimate sharing and fascinating conversation, sweet-talking me into believing he is the man of my dreams. I tell Josh he and I are no longer right for each other, and we discuss our ending for hours until we agree our conflicts are insurmountable. But, returning from a modeling job, I open the front door to Josh seated on my leg-less chair, crying and clutching my bed pillow to his chest. I am unmoved. Josh moves out.

Perhaps it is Josh's anguish that will evoke my need to live alone awhile before I decide if I want to live with the "man of my dreams." In that moment, Rob's faults will be clear to me. And here is the moment, the dichotomy, so hard to understand. For a year, Rob will alternate cleverly-reasoned guilt trips with passionate love trips, until he convinces me that I cannot live without him.

In my last days of freedom in the living room, Billie Holiday's 1950s gravelly voice, like hopelessness and heroin, sings another woman's nightmare:

> …but I love him.
> I don't know why I should,
> He isn't true,
> He beats me, too,
> What can I do?

I will never be hit, and will not know for eighteen years that, all the same, this is domestic violence. Full of compassion, my arms will hold Rob in the living room as he sobs his despair over his problems, as he croons romance like the 1940's movie musicals we become glued to.

Twenty-five years must pass before, alone and free at last, I travel a thousand miles from my new home in Oregon back to Los Angeles to drive past the renovated stucco triplex, viewing from the outside the now uncovered windows that belong to strangers.

My heart will tighten as once again I feel the time machine surge forward, the boards being hammered up over the windows, the room plunged into darkness, my thoughts battered into confusion – clack, clack, clack.

And now, my mind reenters the living room to tear off the foil, drag down the dust-saturated curtains, and open the windows. Sunlight dances across my body, lighting up my face in multi-colored vibrancy. It splashes the air with Shakuhachi flute music, Celtic folk tunes, Native American chants, Chinese pipa improvisations, and African drums. My heart leaps with the sunlight over walls and rug, until I sit down in a chair that has all four legs and, loud as I can, I sing.

A Fair Heart
Jenny L. Rife

I'll swear on your Bible and my first edition Capote
That we're all right and all wrong for each other.
Your jeweled cross outdazzles my iron monkey,
Your thoroughbred beats my carousel pony,
Your torch eclipses my tealight.
Your money clip, my penny jar.
Your cannonball, my shooting star.
Be with me
And I'll play you a symphony on my hurdy gurdy,
Pin a hothouse dandelion on your tuxedo,
Pop the cork on a bottle of spring rain.
Your aria, my lullaby.
Your know-it-all, my wonder-why.
I'll trade my cowboys for your kings,
My veranda for your empire,
My thistle for your fleur-de-lis.
Your mockingbird, my paper crane.
Your rocket ship, my paper plane.
Your reverence, my sacrilege.
Your sentiment, my burning bridge.

Bloom

It is not my memory, but my mother's
The first time I charmed a man in the back seat of a car
He was pumping gas, we eyed each other
Through the streaked rear window
I am told I brandished my dimples shamelessly
He took my mother's wrinkled dollars, said,
That little one's been kissed by the Blarney Stone
She took it for a blessing, this gentle mangling
My gifts bloomed like fountain mallow
On back roads, in back seats
Perfumed with sweat and gasoline
Rotted leaves and blackberry wine
One boy at a time

Spotless Day
Kathleen Haley

When January coaxes
me to believe
I may sow rows
of snow peas

I unfurl pillow
cases from the washer,
pin them to the clothesline,
the flannel imbued
with wind and sun.

Flags of hope
for this spotless day
wave to the clouds.

I plug in the iron
when the cotton
is almost dry

and press
God's breath
into the cloth

savor the removal
of each wrinkle.

When the steam
Issues
my hair curls

conjuring sumptuous
dreams
of spring.

Wildflower
Wanda Lea Brayton

Jagged edges of parchment torn with worry and etched
in current's sultry song
leave feathery fibers dusting the surface of an ancient desk;
the ruins of a life well-lived, the flow of infinite dreams.

You pressed me between forgotten pages edged in guilt,
a rose paled by time, not understanding I had blooms left
to offer to one without memories of thorns.

You finally thought to open the book, stunned by the single petal
I left behind.

I curled myself into the ragged edges of feverish silence,
fetal with ferocious sorrows I could not seem to elude,
even in slumber.

I linger in shadow's peripheral glance, trying to see
without being seen -
listen without being heard –
as this furious tide engulfs me within its wild wrath.

My strength wanes as the riptides grip me
from the loving grasp of arms that would hold me -
that would save me from myself.

There's a hole in my breast
where once a heart rhythmed its way beyond pluralistic Eden -
now, only echoes of gaping wounds remain,
scars etching skin towards invisible sunlight.

I am not as I once was,
nor am I as I will be.

Seeds germinate within, roots seeking deeper soil to adhere to
and bloom something new from ancient grief.

Captured by shallow breath, eyes glazed with trust and terror,
I shall shed this flesh that haunts.

Blood Moon
Lori Kagan

As you rise
over West 55th Street
oddly immense
red as the rocks
of Sedona

I'm struck
with the urge
to bow down

beg you
to grant me

the power
to enchant rush hour
multitudes

make them stop
in their tracks

notice my
existence too

for just a few
moments

Evanescence
Justin Rogers

You were right here.
It was you.
You stole my dreams, again.
Shifted somehow, like always,
but it was you.

This time,
your hair was different,
not the right red.
Your face, still pretty,
was less wholesome.
Even the shape of your body had changed.
Not as feminine, or genuine.
Thinner, as if you were fading away.

Your eyes,
like all the times before,
were the same.
Your eyes.

Your eyes haunt me.
Beseeching windows,
I cannot see through.
Sending messages,
I fail to grasp.

We walked side by side,
separated by oceans.
Heads tilted, faces turned,
unable to touch.

It was you.
You were right here.
I could feel your music.
Your spirit was in your song.

You are all around me.
A scent
in a hallway
of my mind.

Of Dogs and Men

once there was a man
who had a dog
a good dog   a mutt
smart   loyal   loving

when the dog got old
old and sick
she went off
by herself
to die

they never did find that dog

was she being helpful
right up to the end
or was she only ashamed

perhaps she needed just
   peace and quiet

and many years later
when the man died
alone on the floor
in a room of his home

they sent him to a taxidermist
and carried his things to a curb
all but the dignity
which they couldn't find

i'm not old or sick
or maybe i am but
i wish i could just
    disappear

like that dog

A Glance
Ann Minoff

A glance
A half-nosed insubstantial glance
A twist
A turn
A half-sensed, half-felt twist

A word
A secondary incorrectly spelled word
And then a breath
In my hand my fleshy warmly particled hand

A secret wish
My unsaid terrifying wish
To know that God
The unrivaled, unpretentious power of God
Resides within
This insignificant row of twenty-four ribs

Breathing in
Breathing out
The remarkable presence of almighty God

Rejoice

Sometimes my head drops
to the ground
and becomes silent
out of weariness

Inside I sense
a dark vastness
searing across violet hills
spread out against a multitude of stars

What if I am
tied by subtle threads
to everyone
experiencing the same weariness

And as I lift my eyes
determined
to recount the vastness
to remember who I am
to rejoice once again

Each one connected to each one
spread out against the multitude of stars
rejoices together

The Jeweler's Son
Paul Weidknecht

Wyatt Earp never wore makeup, but as the woman ran that foam wedge thing across Ray's forehead, he also realized the lawman had never been on television either. So sitting in his small back office, a pair of paper napkins tucked into his collar as a bib, Ray decided to let this woman finish what she needed to finish. He wouldn't tell these people their business; they knew television and he knew jewelry.

The door chime rang yet again and Ray peeked sideways toward the front. Fifty times the chime had rung that morning and fifty times he'd glanced toward the door, a habit turned reflex for most city jewelers he knew. A full shop always made him a little nervous, especially when he was unable to see the whole showroom and counter. Closed-circuit security monitors on his desk helped with the basic view, but they were no substitute for face-to-face, flesh and blood eyeballing. However, he'd closed the shop for the interview today, feeling confident that anyone now entering was part of the production crew and not here to kill him.

Ray flexed his calf against the ankle holster that carried the hold-out piece, an old Smith & Wesson .38 snub his father kept near the office safe for the forty-one years he ran the shop. He didn't need the gun right now, but carrying it had become another of those habits turned reflex, its weightiness a secret comfort when so many others things in life had failed to live up to their promise. Recalling the one time his father had the chance to use it, Ray frowned to himself, shook off the thought, and continued watching the people around him.

Crew members squeezed past him, carrying light stands, microphones, and coils of electrical cord, and Ray thought it odd to see strangers milling around his office as if they'd always known the place. A pony-tailed producer wearing a Yankees cap pulled down over his eyes walked by in quick step, pointing toward Ray's shirt, giving a thumbs up, an approval of his earlier suggestion for Ray to lose the suit jacket and show off the hardware—his 1911 Model Colt .45—and tooled leather shoulder holster like an old movie detective. Maybe like Sam Spade or one of those guys, he'd said.

This company had been here five years earlier when they'd filmed the first documentary. Afterwards, they mailed him several copies which he'd either handed out to friends or misplaced. Over the years he'd seen it on a cable channel that broadcast police chases, courtroom brawls, and soccer stadium riots, always at two or three in the morning. He wasn't crazy about the vigilante angle they'd taken for the program, and he'd spoken to these people about it, but in the end they deferred to folks in a skyscraper far away whom they claimed had the final say on marketing.

"They want me to go light on the concealer over that," the woman said softly, motioning with her pinky toward the scar on his scalp. "I didn't want you to think I missed it. By the way, I like your shirt."

Puckered and shiny, the scar was a nickel-sized divot off to the right and just in front of his receding gray hairline. Ray understood why they'd want to keep the scar visible, its origin surely part of the sequel they were filming today. "Why, thank you. I just bought it," he said.

Ray looked down at the backs of his hands. Blue veins wormed under the skin, their bulges running over and through the knuckles' rises and valleys, and several liver spots seemed darker than usual. Fifty-eight looked more like seventy-eight. Casual observers might have thought them the kind to carve a mallard from a cedar block or tie a Royal Coachman, assuming them gentle, even grandfatherly.

Ray had killed four people. Three armed robbers and a guy who wanted revenge for his stone-dead buddy. All straight-up heist guys, not a diamond switching slickster or grab and run punk among them. All shot, all dead, each a center mass or head shot from the front. Wounding and arrest hadn't figured into the process. Each incident had been classified as justifiable homicide due to self-defense, and Ray never spent a day in jail, never got close to pulling down a prison term. That's what the first documentary was about: the old jeweler, Raymond Castle, who had killed four men in three separate incidents, the guy who had guns everywhere around the shop—the .45 he always wore, the .40 Glock in a compartment under the counter, the Remington pump-action12-gauge in the back, and the other half dozen or so he hadn't mentioned—the guy who neighboring store owners praised before police investigators and television reporters, sent lunch over to, called Wild Ray, and, yes, sometimes Wyatt Earp.

They'd also mentioned in the documentary the time he put in at the firing range. Two hours a night, three times a week, at least. More on the weekends, with Saturdays and Sundays each four-hour affairs. As Ray liked to say: good hadn't happened by accident.

Still, he couldn't help but recall the irony of it; the same practice that saved his life had destroyed his marriage, as Lydia, a patient woman who had become rightly jealous over paper targets and clay pigeons, packed up their twins and headed to a safer place, a small town in central Nebraska where armed robberies almost never happened and guns were used for hunting. He and the girls corresponded for two years, but after Lydia remarried their communication became less, until the only mail he could expect from them was a Christmas greeting and a generic convenience store birthday card, nothing personalized about either except the signatures.

And now this company was here again because he had killed two more people, managing to get himself shot in the head at the same time. Ray wondered if there was enough material for a new show. Sure there was a new audience after five years, but he wasn't certain that two more bodies and Cameron Barrow's bad aim justified a second-go-round.

"Yes, that's true," Ray told the interviewer, a professional, serious-looking woman in her thirties. "My father owned the shop for forty one years and never drew his gun."

39

"But he was robbed once," she said.

"Yes, we were robbed in 1958."

"It's interesting that you say 'we', because I understand you actually were *here*, in this shop with your father when that robbery took place. You were eight years old at the time."

"After school, instead of walking back home, I would visit my father. I'd do little jobs for him, taking out the garbage, cleaning the showcase glass, stuff like that. The shop was empty that afternoon. A man rushed in with a revolver, forcing my father to crouch down and open the safe. The guy was never caught."

"And where were you when this happened?"

For the past fifteen minutes she had asked different sorts of questions, easy ones about background, interests, hobbies; personal information to be used for a profile. Now the lights around him seemed warm and Ray reached down, picking up a glass of water he'd placed on the carpet at his feet. He took a sip and replaced it. "I was kneeling next to him."

Ray noticed the interviewer's eyes narrow. She brought the pen down slowly, placing it across the yellow ledger pad on her lap. Folding her hands, she waited a moment.

"It's still difficult to speak about to this day, isn't it?"

Before this interview, Ray imagined what he would say, all the things he hadn't thought of during the first interview, clever lines he'd roll off, tough guy talk too good to leave on the cutting room floor: *The robber sets his terms, then I enforce mine.* Or: *They think about robbing me, and when it's all over they're not even thinking.* And to those who would rob him, his favorite: *Stop at the door before you become a doorstop.*

Now there was nothing. Witty phrases log-jammed in his mind and he became quiet, stalled in thoughts decades old. Her question hadn't thrown him—they'd brought up the '58 robbery in the first documentary—but his reaction had, and he was surprised. She was good, this interviewer, sensing another story, veering from the script to get at something deeper. She was right, it was difficult to speak about, but not in the way she thought. The interviewer hadn't seen it all, because if she had she would've realized that somebody

40

who had taken a .32 slug in the head and put six people under dirt wouldn't have nightmares about some half-century old heist. So he said, yes, it is difficult, even today, knowing he was telling the truth and lying in the same breath.

"About this latest incident," she began. "Two men tried to rob you and you killed both in the attempt. However, one of them shot you."

Ray tilted his head, pointing to the scar. "Yeah. Right here. Bullet ran across my scalp, stuck in the wall behind me. A lot of blood, but nothing life-threatening."

"You must have thought you were dying?"

As a kid, Ray remembered a man his father had hired as part-time help—War Hero Joe, Ray called him—who told of a forehead wound he'd received at Omaha Beach that made him think a piece of German shrapnel had blinded him from the amount of blood that had run into his eyes. That's what Ray had thought, that he'd been blinded. Death hadn't come to mind. But his lawyer had told him on more than one occasion that favorably adjudicated self-defense shootings always included a properly expressed fear of death.

"Yes, I thought I was going to die," he said.

He could have gone on, describing more, giving these people the drama they needed to keep viewers awake at two or three in the morning, but now he didn't even feel like finishing the interview. He wanted them out of here and short answers would hurry things up. He knew it didn't matter what he said; any gaps would be filled in later with images of red and blue lights flashing against yellow crime scene tape, black and white stills of bodies on his floor, the lack of color making the shootings seem less real and more ghastly at the same time.

"With all of the robberies you've endured, have you ever wondered why they keep happening to you? Do you ever ask, 'Why me?'"

He had wondered. Six bodies in sixteen years. Whole police forces hadn't killed that many people in a century. Why had this kept happening? He'd speculated about the reasons: drugs, gangs, moral

41

decay, even the challenge of taking out the gunslinger jeweler, but none of it sufficiently explained why he was the one being robbed while the other jewelers in the city went about safely running their businesses.

"I'd have to say I'm unlucky," he said. "But if I could add something—."

"Of course."

"I'm not sorry I killed them. Any of them. And I'll never be. I was defending my life and property, a right to which everyone is entitled. What I'm sorry about is that any of it *happened*, that events came together, in their lives and mine, to cause these things to occur. They could have gone their ways, I could have gone mine. They would not be dead and I would not be the reason."

"But isn't that reality?" she asked, less gently than he'd expected.

"One I live with every day."

The interview continued for another hour, and when it finally ended, the interviewer smiled tightly, shook his hand, and quickly walked outside for a cigarette. Ray saw her through the front show window on the sidewalk, staring uptown into the wind, a shake of her head now and then to keep the hair from her face. One of the producers handed him a business card, mentioning something about calling if he had anything to add. Ray noticed the card had three phone numbers on it, and reflexively he began to speak, but decided against it; more talk wasn't going to accomplish a thing and it would just keep them here longer. The crew finished packing in a fraction of the time it had taken to set up and before Ray knew it, he was alone.

Sitting in the office, he flicked the card onto the desk, hitched his tie away from his throat, and released the collar button. They'd been here all morning and his head hurt. With the toe of his shoe, he reached out and closed the office door, eager to get out of these clothes he'd bought specially for today. Buying them seemed wasteful now, nice shirt compliment aside. He reached down, lifted the leg of his pants, and unstrapped his ankle holster to start changing. He tried recalling what he'd told them, not sure if he had revealed too much, but now he was drained and distracted, his mind crowded with other matters. Yet he was certain of one thing: there would never be another interview.

Ray pulled through the gates, past the three-foot high chain-link fence that surrounded Riverwood Cemetery. The grass had greened-up from a rainy spring and the dogwood blossoms had exploded on every branch, creating a wall of white that stretched across the far end of the cemetery property. The mingled scent of various flowers moved lightly on the breeze, swirling inside the open window of his car. A man who looked to be in his eighties leaned over a long-handled pump, priming it with water from a coffee can. He wore baggy dress pants held up by suspenders and a white shirt with the sleeves rolled to his elbows. He spotted Ray and stared, then waved and turned back to his work. Ray returned his wave and headed toward the rear of the cemetery.

Ray's lawyer had told him on several occasions never to visit the graves of anyone he'd killed. He'd told Ray that if he were ever photographed there, it might show remorse and possibly open the door for a civil suit. They could even call it harassment, say he was tap dancing on somebody's grave. Worse than this, he'd said, Ray might run into a member of the family.

The narrow gravel road curved tightly around the plots, and the small headstone appeared twenty-five feet way. He put the car into park, turned off the ignition and sat for a moment. After glancing into each of the mirrors, he stepped out.

Recently, someone had planted a cluster of red and yellow tulips at the base of the stone, the palm prints still visible in the soil where it had been packed down. Ray's eyes came up to the birth year, 1990. An acidic sensation bolted through his stomach. He'd known Derek's age from police reports, from newspapers, but there was something jarring about seeing this engraved here, marked out in such permanence. To Ray, nineteen-ninety was yesterday.

He looked again at the flowers. A photograph wrapped in plastic sat behind them on the base. Ray leaned over and picked it up.

43

Moisture had gotten inside and beads of condensation clung to the plastic. Without looking any closer, he knew what the picture would show: three or four people in a living room, arms around each other's shoulders, smiling in front of a mantle or fireplace, the harsh flash from the camera reflecting in the mirror behind them. This was Derek before it all, no thoughts of robbery, no fears of death; a person in happier times, a family intact.

The names of the six came to him. It was impossible not to know the names; they had become unforgettable. Just as he had ended their lives, they had ruined his. Everyone had lost. He lingered on the last two names and thought of the scene he had kept from the interviewer.

Cameron Barrow raising the muzzle of that .32 over the edge of the Rolex showcase. Ray with the Glock already in his hand below the counter, bringing it up, zeroed in on the space between the *8* and *1* on Cameron's football jersey. Ray dipping a second, Cameron firing. The sound, a compact deafening pop, followed by another. Ray's head jerking back, the *1* disappearing for a second on Cameron's turn, Ray's bullet on its way through the top hole in the *8*.

Barrow dropping, his hand hitting the frame of the showcase on the fall. The revolver clattering onto the glass top, spinning a half-turn. Ray on the floor behind the counter, leaning on his elbow, pushing himself up, Derek Nathan running for the door, his feet slipping from under him. Blood running from Ray's scalp down into his eyes, a flash recollection of War Hero Joe, then the rest of Joe's story, backhanding the blood from his eyes, focus blurred, but glorious French sand in sight. And Ray blinking away the blood, a reckoning in sight.

Derek unable to open the door, the brass knob slick with his sweat. Ray around the counter, a quick glance at Cameron, who doesn't move and looks like he won't. Derek giving up on the door, wheeling around with his gun, and Ray on him, aiming, bracketing the front post sight inside the *U*-shaped rear one.

And then Ray's wish, an imagination: Derek, nineteen, holding his palms out, as if waiting to receive a blessing; his gun

absent, a figment of blood and emotion. Ray reading his face, reaching out, helping him to his feet. *I know, Derek. You made a mistake. You got mixed up in this thing and made a mistake, is all. But you won't have to pay for it with your life. I promise. You'll reach forty or fifty and look back and realize what could've happened and you'll be thankful. So, go, take this gift, this blessing, and live. Just live.*

With the city almost two hours behind him, Ray continued on the interstate, the tandem thump of tires over the concrete joints rhythmic and familiar. Beech-maple forests flanked the highway, and when the land opened for the river's flood plain or a farmer's field, the vista revealed one rounded mountain folding seamlessly into the next as if a single verdant blanket had been thrown over all of it. Seven miles later he exited, stopped at the blinking red light, and headed up toward the lake.

He always liked this road, especially as a kid. The jostling from the high crown and patched asphalt signaled the awaiting excitement in ways the interstate's smooth monotony could never conjure, as if the road were designed to wake dozing adventurers at exactly the right moment so they wouldn't miss anything. Sometimes on the way up to the cabin they'd pull over to get some sweet white corn from a roadside stand, or if they had gotten the place in late August, they'd stop at the mountainside orchard to buy peaches. Once, when they had left later than usual and dusk had already begun, they saw a black bear sow and a pair of cubs emerge from the orchard and cross in front of them. To Ray, the trip started when his father turned onto this road, and no sooner.

The cabin was a rental, a place owned by Mrs. Newell, an elderly, long-time customer whose praise of his father's work in restoring a family heirloom bordered on homage. She never charged them, saying they could have the whole month of August every year if they wanted, but they only ever took two weeks a season. Several years later when she died, her son put the place up for sale and quickly got his price from a family who owned a home on the west shore. When Ray's father inquired about the possibility of seasonal

45

renting, the new owners explained it had been purchased for their daughter and her family to be renovated and enlarged into a year-round residence.

The lake appeared, shimmering silver under the afternoon sun. White cabins dotted the far hillside and Ray noticed the small burst of light from a windshield as a car across the lake wound its way around the shoreline drive. He recalled how relaxed his father seemed while at the lake house, as he called it, and how, except for his annual but sincere acknowledgment of Mrs. Newell's generosity and its origin, he never spoke about the shop while up in the mountains. Ray spotted the house up ahead, slowed down, and parked to the side. He walked down toward the water.

The cabin had been neither renovated nor enlarged, but razed and replaced by this home. Down the hill in back, the floating dock bobbed gently, looking the same as when they'd vacationed here those years ago and when they'd spread his father's ashes here that mild day last October with the maples orange all around them. The owners told him he was welcome here anytime he ever needed to think. Don't even knock, just go down there, they'd said.

Ray walked onto the dock and stared at the spot where he'd seen the breeze push his father's ashes across the water last fall.

He saw them kneeling at the safe, his father fretful, trying to concentrate, thinking through the lefts and the rights on the combination dial. His father was saying please, please. Soon the pleads dissolved from shaky words into a stream of whimpering sounds. The man reached out, grabbed his father's hair, and banged his head into the steel door. His father grimaced, then began to sob, the first of three times Ray would ever witness this in his life, as the robber's knife—there was never a revolver—stayed pressed to Ray's throat.

Still on his knees, his father filled the man's brown paper bag with the money and gems. The robber's look of disgust signaled the emergence of something inside, a rage that simple theft couldn't satisfy, and everything in his life he'd been unable to do to others he did then. The man stomped his father's face, pinning him to the floor

46

under his shoe. Without touching skin, the robber slit his father's shirt up the back, and still holding the knife, reached in with both hands and tore the shirt open to each side. He cut away two strips of cloth and threw them onto the floor, making his father put them with the money and gems, spitting on him as he reached down and snatched up the bag.

Ray remembered wondering why his father hadn't followed the plan. Hunched over the safe, he was supposed to arrive at the last number, pull on the handle, and hitch a moment, pretending the door heavier and the hinge stiffer than they really were. He was to shield his right hand with his body, reach under the safe, tear away the .38 snub taped there. Then he was to make sure his finger was inside the trigger guard, turn and put a bullet through the guy's brain. He was supposed to fight.

Ray recalled how he'd found ways to avoid the shop after school, how he'd told his friends it had been a gun and not a knife, that the newspapers had gotten it wrong. Later, as a teenager, he thought also how that robber had changed their relationship, that over time the misjudgment of a kid had hardened into something unrecognizable and impenetrable that neither of them could identify or break apart. When Ray came to work full-time in the shop after graduating from high school, it seemed as if the two hardly spoke, each moving sullenly from office to counter and back again until his father turned the shop over to him twenty-three years later.

One thought gave rise to the next and Ray pondered for a moment how his father had become known for creating beautiful things that gave people joy, while he was known for ending lives that gave others misery; the father dealing in gold rings, the son in brass casings.

Ray looked up from the water.

As sensitive as the past now seemed, he knew it also had become understandable. Time had explained many things, and years later when his daughters were born, Ray understood what his father had done. He wasn't a coward. In fact, he was just the opposite. Ray realized his father never feared for himself, that the plan to go for the gun was on only if he were alone, and that humiliation is a bargain, a trade easily made, when a loved one's life is at stake.

It was time to leave, and Ray knew it always had been. He couldn't dwell on the realities of what had happened or on the impossibilities of an unrealized past, of how his life might have turned out with better understanding or deeper insight, because something was up ahead, past the counter and beyond the sound of the door chime. He knew Dad would have understood.

Ray walked back across the boards, ripples spreading from under the dock, the hollow slap of water against wood. Then he stopped. He flexed his calf again to be certain. The .38 snub was gone, left back at the office when he had changed clothes, and as Ray thought of this, and of a new beginning, he smiled into the warmth of the day and to the humanity of his forgetfulness.

Northern Anniversary
Stephen Massimilla

Willow banks of Scotland are phantom fountains
thinned in wind; coal-black spires of Glasgow
still whispering near stacks, hills and mountains
mooned in green haloes, the last sky now

behind us. Blue mist fills our quiet terrace
as we stare down toward a blooded maze of walls
under bells that cloak the orange sun in blackness.
Friend to itself, but otherwise odd, what appalls

is her whisper: it is sober, and the gas lamps
float in schools—no hopes, no flagrant dead.
I wish I could tell her that what stamps

out the fire was wine that had gone . . . to her head
and so remind us: don't survive. Relax,
as winter closes in behind our backs.

The Birthday
Karen Holmberg

The wild mum's violet petals
   cringe inward like a touched
   anemone as a flame from
the candle we've embedded
     in the glazy custard of your tart
does a scare dance on the vase's globe, and
the cranberry wax fogs over
      as if perspiring. We are all
   shy with wonder, giggling

and giddy, shuddering in first plunge
   of chill water as you show us
   how to pass
a finger through the flame.
     We shiver because two
charismata meet, both
with the power to destroy. And though
     you mock the flame as you mock
   us all, pranking yet tender,

assured of possession, the truth is
   you're in thrall to us and so you need
   to make us feel at once
our beauty and our foolishness. *See, hold*
     your palm above it and YAH!

But pass your finger quickly through
it . . . and here your finger gives
          the flame a few dapper slaps,
     kid glove to an insubordinate cheek. The flame

winces then stretches back
     taller than before, and again
     you smart it, curling your forefinger
round its neck like
          a shepherd's crook to pull it off
its stage. The lip of flame quivers
as we all take turns, even
               little Lily, her shiver-laugh
     of bravado bolstered to aplomb,

sniffing her finger for its sheath
     of soot.
     Angel-beautiful, flowing
in an upward stream,
          the flame set dancing in all
your lively eye-lights bends
and parts where I touch it, draws up
               again healed and whole.
     Love, deal gently with us.

That Life
Robert King

The life you thought was yours
has walked off down the railroad track.

Oh, not like the hoboes you waved to
in the passing box-cars but the boy

that walked the rails after the train passed,
heading toward his life beside the creek

that trickled under the shaggy trestle
and swam through grass before the highway.

He dreamed in the current's hush and flow
but couldn't remember what when he woke up.

If waking up is what, years later, he did.
Now in the suburb of a vanquished farm

you sit and wonder about that boy—
what could he possibly have been thinking

all those summer afternoons—and what
is he thinking now, having gotten up

and started back, that boy who never wondered
where the train, the creek, where even he, was headed.

Your X
Arthur Gottlieb

marks the spot
you first met,
a bloody bull's eye
now for her rage.

At the moment
she's scavenging
the old closets
for skeletons,
heaped helter-skelter
in chaotic cellar & attic.

Rattling bracelets
like shaman witch bones
she invokes the divinity
of her planned punishment.

No stopping her. Even
wind can't slow her
momentum. She's backing
a rented flatbead up
to your front door,
hoping to cart your broken
heart to her doll hospital.

She wants to mend wounds
with her needles & thread
the sad story of her life
thru the gutless folds
of your sick stomach.

She's saving her sewing
kit & scissors to shape
man-eating flowers out of
her skin petals, tiger
lilies that could claw
a man's remorse raw.

Careful, she means to
jack up the foundation,
disconnect the plumbing,
sever the main artery
to your heart's desire,
before building a fire under
your martyred feet, until
you admit she's the one
woman you should have gladly
                    died for.

Unattributed
Robert H. Guard

You will not find this painting
In a museum or gallery.

It is composed on the back of a man's skull,
Inside, where he mixes his colors.

The metal gate stands, resolute
In the sunset's rust. Above,

Black birds fly without a name,
Like salt shaken over the shoulder.

The sky holds its clouds like children
From the unbroken sky below.

There is nothing here, nothing to take
For the taking. So you wait

With the blue mirror and the man,
To be released.

Pebbles in the Road
W.K. Lawrence

Subtle arrangements
Of rain etching prints
On oily ground
Steam rising
Birds speaking
In tongue
Of nature and sex
A single sound wave
Shakes the house
Under shattered moon
Light falls on all sides
On friend and foe
With ravenous voracity
That grasps and guts
The insides with rippled rhythms
Bending particles
Lingering memories
Of the moments just before a storm.

Out of this World

Exhale the red smoke through your nose
Let it funnel up into the wheel
That turns in the sky like a Beatles song
From when Jesus still walked the Earth
From the cavemen who invented
Troubles, books, and plagues
To the modern men who invented
Toll booths and more plagues
The smoke will always be the same
Drifting up up up and away
And never coming back down.

Sleep Walking
Renee Emerson

My mother tells me a story where the winter
came calling and my aunt slept down
the hallway. The door racking against its frame,
cold air, stars, concrete a cool kiss on her
bare feet in this delicious striding-sleeping. Yes, I've been lost
before, like a little cat, mewing my way home before anyone
could find me. I've been put back to bed in good ways,
smothered in blankets like a casserole. At times the night-winter
huffs against the window panes, and they heave a little,
being poorly made, and the radiator knocks to keep
me placed, the winter cooing for a sidle up to my cheeks,
a curl up in my outstretched hand as I sleep.

Gray
Rebecca Foust

was the color of your hair, soft gunmetal glint
like the mill steel cord-stacked in girders
at the railroad repair yard, gray like
the library façade, limestone so soot-soaked
it looked like metal, gray like
the man's hankie you wore to school, a bandit,
running past the mills where your father

learned to lay brick and set stone. He taught
you how to canoe the river, turn handsprings
and skate backwards better than any boy.
You watched him diminish and dim into
his rocking chair, crying just once, when
that fool kid killed the hawk that had cut
dips and arcs into his twilights.

Your face suffused with the glow of snow bank
bonfires, you skated backwards holding my hands
so I could skate forwards. We dipped and arced,
etched the dark ice. You taught me how to feather
a stroke, swim the width of the warm, brown river.
But it got you too, the lung sickness furnace
reduced you to prime number purity.

I watched you diminish and dim, sunset
leaching into sepia night; twilight
caught in the net of your long, gray lashes.
Your feet, fingertips, then your sweet face
drained. All of you gone
but these few bits of bone
left sifting your body, your ashes.

Objects
Raymond Luczak

The rest of us, disposed of in a dump,
await the day, as seagulls and flies flit
and feast on rotting scraps and carcasses,
when we are no longer made and ignored.
Remaindered, we tell the same old story:
The mighty dollar can wreak the order
of all that Mother Nature had decreed.
We will canvass the sweet blanket of death,
oozing toxins from our decayed bodies,
once engineered to visual perfection
and celebrated in magazine ads,
with methane steaming upwards to the skies.
Long after they've perished from making us,
we shall inherit the earth with silence.

The Cloud Walker
Ben E. Campbell

It wasn't until I moved out West two years ago, right after I let loose of everything that held me upright and packed my belongings in a small pickup truck, that I discovered the greatest truth of my life: I can walk on clouds. Sometimes I mean this figuratively, but most of the time I'm talking in the physical sense, like an angel. Or a pilot. Or someone stuck in purgatory.

I'm a beam walker for a construction company in one of the West's growing metropolitans. We bolt and bind horizontal steel girders seventy-five stories in the air, a thousand feet up. Megastructures, we call them. It isn't really the kind of occupation you'd come to expect for a thirty-two-year-old flatlander with a profile like mine: tall and clumsy, notoriously known for having two left feet—the kind of guy that once had to be talked down from a single-level rooftop when cleaning out the gutters. I grew up in Winston-Salem, North Carolina, and the only climbing I ever did there was up apple trees on my granddaddy's tobacco farm. Out here though, I'm a whole different person. I'm starting a brand new life.

And the pay is good as well. With the money I'm putting back there's no telling how soon I'll set things straight, how soon I'll get back home. That is, if ever I'm welcomed. But thinking like that does no good, so it's better to count my blessings.

I live in a camper on the outskirts of town. Bought it for a grand from a guy outside of Albuquerque, when I was working my way out here. The land I squat on belongs to the government but in two years' time no one's said much about it. Perhaps Uncle Sam doesn't care now that he's no longer using it for testing Stealth fighters and such. Either way it's an o.k. setup, me alone at night with just the stars and darkened mountains, a few coyote calls to cover the sound of my heart.

Through the day I've got the crew I work with. Most of them are Navajo Indians come over from the rez to make some steady bank. They're a fearless bunch who could easily climb to the moon. The foremen think they do this work to strut their courage, convince themselves they haven't lost touch with their past. But that's just stupid white people talk. Like anybody else, they just want to pick up a paycheck on Friday, maybe take their gals out for a movie and see what's happening on the town. They invite me to come along but I never accept. I don't want to feel like a third wheel messing up their ground time. Plus they don't know about my wife, the one back East who refuses to take my calls. Only Earl knows about her.

Earl's the lone black guy on our crew, a native Arizonian with a bent for pondering life's questions. We get along real well, though it wasn't always that way. When I first got hired on he didn't much trust me, what with me being Southern and all and him thinking that we're all the same: a bunch of cross-burning, black-hating rednecks. He made it clear to me the first time we shared a beam together. He said, "Look here, Johnny Reb. You think I'm dumb enough to look away from you up here then you got another thing coming. You're not gonna make some brown spot of me with a shove in the back!"

It threw me through a loop, the way he just came out with it like that, and for a good long minute I leaned against an upright thinking of how I should respond. I wanted to tell him I was a Democrat, that my mother's side of the family had fought for Lincoln's North, that, heck, the best man in my wedding had been a black guy. Everything I thought of though seemed like stupid white people talk so in the end I just chuckled and said, "Well, you've got another thing coming if you think I'm gonna let you pull a walk-by on me, Mister gang banger."

Fortunately, Earl saw the humor in my stupid attempt and shook my hand right there. We've been best buds ever since.

Earl comes out to the camper a lot on weeknights. After a long, hard day of beam bolting we build a campfire and sit out in the dirt with our legs crossed, sometimes talking, sometimes staring into

63

the flames. Reconnecting ourselves to the ground we've come to loathe.

For Earl it's a chance to reflect on the philosophy books he's been reading. He goes on about titles like *Man's Search for Meaning* and *Beyond Good and Evil*. Really out there stuff. Metaphysical, he calls it. I want to tell him to stay away from that voodoo, that too much thinking will only turn him into a mad man, but I'm no one to be preaching, really. On the nights I've drunk too much I open up like a wind pocket and spill my sappy guts about things beyond my control. I've told Earl a lot that way. From my failings as a husband to my deepest, darkest fears. I just wish I were able to speak so freely with my wife. It gets rough most days, feeling the way I do, holding all this in. Not even Earl knows the real depths of my pain, and for that there's a method to my madness. If I told him, he'd alert the foremen, and they would ground me quick, cut me from the crew. There's no tolerance for head cases, not when there are safety goals to meet.

A life on the level. I could never do that again—not even if I somehow make it home. Maybe there is work like mine in Memphis, Charlotte, or Atlanta. Some place in the South branching up, rather than out. That could buy me time, another chance to show my strength, and Lord only knows that I need to flaunt my courage. It could be the dealmaker that mends my broken marriage.

Speaking of, my wife's name is Patricia. She's from West Virginia, has long, black hair and an accent like rain water tapping a tin bucket. We met on North America's oldest river, the New River, ten years ago, on a warm autumn day, when her canoe front collided with mine between a narrow row of rocks. I had seen it coming from at least a mile away. As I labored beneath a tree-filled canvas, fighting the rushing rapids, this sleek, tan Kevlar bounced right in my path. Of course, I could have let it miss me, but its captain was such a looker, so beautiful with all her fight, that I had to let it happen. It was like destiny, her crashing into me.

"I'm so sorry," is all she said, then, and again, when we had paddled along the bank. I could have shared my wisdom and set the rookie straight. I was a guide in those days, trained in giving lessons, and there was much she had to learn. But all I could muster was "You're absolutely gorgeous." She smiled, my heart went soft, and we finished the voyage together. The rest was for the books.

Within a year we had married and were living in southwest Virginia, near the Carolina border, a middle place between our two families' homes. Life moved slow there and for the most part we liked that. I worked the river and she taught school. We bought a house, went on camping trips, went canoeing. Sometimes we made love in the canoe while floating the gentle stretches, sometimes along the banks. We talked, laughed, cried, bickered, dreamed, hoped, and prayed, all together. It was everything I could have asked for. A real, genuine life.

And then that thing happened. That thing you read about on the second or third page of the newspaper, the unthinkable thing you tell yourself will never happen to *you*.

I think about it a lot when I'm in the air. Sometimes a strong breeze will come along and force me to groping a beam, and in that moment, when my heart is racing and the world below me is nothing more than an anthill beneath my boots, I can feel her leaning into me, the beam standing in her place, in just the same way she did before this thing came between us. Everything is good again; it's like we are back on solid ground. Only it never lasts for long. For as soon as the breeze dies down, I must let go of my grip, return to what is real, and that means me and my lonely life.

I guess it is times like those, those dream times, however farfetched they may seem, that continue to give me hope. They are the reason I can't stop calling. The reason I won't sign the papers.

I did a drastic thing moving West, and something even more drastic once I got here—I swore off the news. No television, no newspapers, nothing. Not even radio! Never mind the fact I was destined to become another uninformed American. I had my sanity to think about—the me, me, me of the equation. And that other thing as well, my ability to walk on clouds.

The last thing you want to think about at a thousand feet in the air are the wars and corporate scandals that make one question existence, unless of course you're Earl. But that's a different story.

As for my own, the short of it is I made this vow with myself and I kept it. I did like all those people who dwell in suburbs and lived my life in the dark, which made things nice for a change, not worrying how long the economy would stand, if Armageddon was on the horizon, if more kids would find themselves corrupted by our nature to thirst for blood.

In my spare time I did a lot of puzzles. I liked the feeling I got when the pieces fit into place, that snapping sensation that sounded so perfect in the silence of my camper. The ones with pictures of mountains and forests were my favorite. They reminded me a lot of where my wife came from and the visits we made to her family on back roads and farms. Unfortunately, they too are a thing of the past; they won't take my phone calls either. It's sorta like I never really existed to them, like I never swept their girl off her feet. I really hate that, but what can I do? One day I'm breaking bread at the in-law's and the next I'm sorting puzzle pieces on a dinner tray made into a table. Life is funny that way. A giant, unforeseen mess.

That's why I eventually switched to chess. I figured it was a lot like when I started walking beams, planning each step in advance, avoiding certain pitfalls. And for the longest time it made for a decent life. Just me and the chess pieces, no news about the airwaves. The sound of emptiness ringing inside my ears.

Then one night Earl made mention of something and my Eden was never the same. At first it was just the usual—Earl rambling off his nonsense, the stuff that I never grasp. He wondered if we weren't shadow creatures, our true selves stationed on a realm above the earth. After all, he said, it would explain our sinful manner. The fact we live in darkness, that we are made of light turned black. Whatever, I thought, and let him carry on. But then his talk soon turned.

I try not to hold it against him, for how could Earl have known? It's not like I ever said: "Don't share the evening news with

66

me, Earl, 'cause it might just drive me mad." The subject didn't help matters. Maybe had the report been on something less personal—say a natural weather disaster or the fall of a Wall Street empire—then things would have turned out different. But that wasn't the case. Another shooting had occurred, only a state over from where we lived. The gunman a tenth grader. Four classmates dead. Thirteen wounded. A community torn apart. It hit too close to home for me, me having *left* my home because of a tragedy much the same.

You see, my wife the school teacher, the woman I love more than mountains or rivers or the beautiful air one breathes, or tries to breathe, when a thousand feet in the air, the puzzle piece that fit my life so well—she was pregnant with our child—seven months pregnant to be exact—and one day, while lecturing her students on their improper use of grammar, noting how the Mexican kids who had moved there with their families to harvest Christmas trees were following the grammatical rules of English better than the native speakers, this skinny, tenth-grade punk jumped from his chair and kicked her square in the stomach. Just like that—up and struck her with a Chuck Liddell-like move he had learned watching Ultimate Fighting Challenge.

The blood poured instantly. By the time the paramedics got to her she was pretty much drained, too weak to walk on her own. It took her ten hours to deliver at the hospital. I will never forget the look on her face when they cut the baby loose. Head cocked to the side, eyes pinched with focus, like she was setting her sights on Jesus. The doctors said she was in shock from the impact of the moment, but I saw it for something else. I knew she was straining to hear our baby's cry, as if before they took him he would bid her one farewell. It was the saddest thing I've witnessed.

That look stayed with her a solid fourteen months.

After it was all over, beyond the funeral with the two-foot casket, my wife's stay in a psych ward, and the hours stuck in quicksand, we learned of the kicker's past. Turns out he had given off warning signs that the school had long ignored: bullying his fellow classmates, plaguing the staff with threats, attempting to build a bomb. The kind of out-there signals that should have earned him a quick expulsion. Only no one paid attention. Not the principals, the school board. Not even the tough-guy sheriff. You would think three arrests and a stint in juvie would raise some big suspicions. But why should they have? A thing like that could never happen in *their* county. Not in good ol' Mayberry, U.S.A.

It was almost like in the War Between the States when General Lee commented on the lawmakers in Richmond. Here he was about to lose his ass to the Yankees and their twice-as-large army and all those Richmond boys wanted to do was crack peanuts and spit tobacco juice. Never mind finding a way to counter the Yankee machine. I guess they figured things would just magically work themselves out. I guess they thought a losing war effort could never happen to *them*. It's funny how history keeps repeating itself in this country, especially in the South.

I ponder things like that sometimes when I'm up there in the sky. About men building towers to heaven or children rising up against their elders or guys like Earl raining on folks' parades. I have no choice but to think about that last one because ever since Earl brought it up I've done nothing else. My once perfect marriage. The punk kid. How unbalanced it all became.

It's like that son of a bitch kicked the life right out of us that day and for what I'll never know. Maybe he was pissed for having too much acne, or for having too few friends, or because his parents wouldn't buy him the latest *Madden*. It's beyond my comprehending, to make sense of reasons like those. When I was a kid you popped your zits and hung out with whoever and there wasn't enough time for playing games because the chores took most of your time. Perhaps I'm just old fashioned to think that way, or the world has changed and left me behind. Either way, who was this kid to take his crap out on us? To drive a wedge between us?

All I know is that I miss my wife like hell. I miss watching her braid her lovely hair. The sound of her gentle breathing. The smell of perfumed skin. The way she drawls her I's out when pronouncing words like *Ice*—all the little things. The things I took for granted. They're gone now and they won't be coming back, at least not anytime soon. No matter how many prayers I make, no matter how many buildings I climb, my wife remains a ghost.

The same holds true in my dreams. Every night it's a similar running—me falling from a building like a stack of tossed-off bricks, spiraling toward the bottom, set to meet my death. On the ground below me I can see my graceful wife. She stands there waiting, arms out, prepared to break my fall. Only I never reach her, for each and every time I meet the seventh story, I wake up in a sweat, unable to end my plight. It's a let down all around, from the incomplete journey to the yearning for my wife. When this happens, I just get up from bed and play myself in chess. The match can go for hours. Until I feel my eyes go cross, or the day begins, whichever comes first. Regardless, it's better than having dreams. Better than feeling airless.

If not for such distractions, then I would probably lose my mind. Thank God there's no more t.v. to watch. I hate the sound of voices.

It's probably worth mentioning that after Earl's visit I did a terrible thing, abandoned my Southern honor. I guess it's questionable as to whether I had any honor left, given the way I handled things back home. But that is for some philosopher like Earl to ponder. The here and now of it is I made an awful goof that could have cost me all my hopes.

It happened like this. One weekend I wandered into town, which was equal to having taken a trip to Mars, the ground as strange and foreign. Life on the level's a lot different than when you view it from the sky. Up there you've got some distance, a little safety from all the mayhem, but on the ground it's total madness. Down low, you're just as vulnerable as all the rest. Just as certain to fall flat on your face. Which is where I was after roaming the city's streets— alone in an alley, watching the busy sidewalks, searching for God knows what.

What I found was a teenager skateboarding. A skinny little feller with pants too big for his butt. He looked like a tenth grader, like the kind of student my wife once had to teach. I stepped out of the darkness and asked him for his name. He didn't answer, just

69

skated around me like a vulture circling death. It weirded me out pretty bad, this kid doing some death dance about me, as if it were a warning of things to come, so I tripped him off his skateboard and watched him spit out teeth. He spat out teeth until the cops arrived, then again, when they stuffed me inside their car. His parents were furious at first but I managed to cool them down. I wrote them a nice-sized check and we reached a fair agreement. They would drop the charges and I would leave their town. Never come back. As simple as that.

In a way I think they were grateful. Five grand buys an awful lot of distractions. Enough I imagine to keep him out their hair. Only the cops seemed keen on my motive. When they asked me why I did it, I told them to break a curse. That sounds like quick-think bunk, but no worse really than the punk's who kicked my wife—a repeated "it made me feel better." He could have at least said the devil made him do it. But no. He was having a bad day, having a bad life. Him and his existential problems.

I often wonder what Patricia does now with her spare time, how *she* processes the divide. A friend of ours says she's gotten into yoga, that she teaches that now, instead of English to high school kids.

I picture her at times sitting leg-wrapped on a mat, her brown eyes stern with focus, lips pressed firmly tight. It's a beautiful sight, my wife the frozen goddess, but it never really keeps. The image tends to remind me: of the classes that we took, the techniques she used to practice, how I coached her by her side. All that breathing in and out.

And when that happens I am thrown back to the past, to the day she cut me off, when she told me to leave her life.

The last time we spoke it was the final thing I heard—the sound of her breath. I could hear it over mine as I tried, with no success, to simply say, "I'm sorry."

Despite my ability to climb great heights, a skill I must believe that most would find courageous, my good bud Earl still thinks that I'm a fake. "This isn't you," he's always saying, as if I'm meant for something else. As if one day I will set down my hard hat and take up some noble cause.

He came up with this crazy idea that I'm suffering from a disorder. Dissociative Fugue, he calls it. It's this occurrence where someone moves off from his home and starts a whole new life, creates a new identity. Maybe some stockbroker type becomes a lounge singer in Vegas. He has everything. A family, a career, a house with two-car garage, but he trades it without a thought. Becomes the next Wayne Newton. Never mind starting a new chapter. This guy writes a completely different book.

Earl says such responses are triggered by traumatic events, that I fit the profile perfect. I say Earl's been diving too deep into philosophy, drowning inside his head.

If anything, I believe my predicament's more along the lines of a fireside story he shared about this Greek god named Sisyphus. Earl does this a lot. He goes on about things like Roman history and epigraphs in books that say, "Who shall bring me to the ground?" and the current day Machiavellians, always adding at the end, "This is stuff about us. They were writing this about *you* and *me*."

It was like that with the Sisyphus guy. According to Earl, he screwed up with the gods and was sentenced to pushing rocks. All day pushing rocks up a tall and lonesome mountain. The catch was he never reached the top; he never met his goal. At the end of each day he was placed back at the bottom for another pointless ascent. And on and on he struggled, the cycle never broken.

It feels like that for me at times. Here I am day after day climbing beam after beam in a fight to reach my son, only when nightfall settles I am forced to come back down. Forced to call it quits.

The ground. Now that's a punishment. Your feet on flattened soil, rooted so far from heaven. The cruelest twist of fate.

I wonder if Earl knows of stories such as that. Stories where a man is stuck in helplessness while his wife attempts to heal, or one where a baby flies to heaven while his father flaps dead wings. If he does, he should keep them to himself. I would hate to be reminded. A setback like that might send me off the edge. It really might. And

71

where would I go then? Back to the home I left behind me? To the wife I pushed away? To a day that finally ends?

Not long after the arrest, some of the Indians from work approached me with an offer to cleanse my soul. The oldest in the group, a cat named Albert Climbing Rock, had heard about my screw up through a friend who owned a scanner. Apparently, I had managed to make big news. "A purification process is in order," he declared. "To rid you of your anguish."

I imagined the events that awaited. There would be old-timers dressed in Indian garb—the beads and feathers, the moccasins and jewels—dancing about a campfire. They would dance and chant and pray to free my hurt. Maybe smoke some kind of pipe. I hungered to see their home.

Instead we went to a bar.

A few drinks in we talked about the cloud walk, the strength we feel when we're up there. How "transcendent", as Earl would put it, one becomes when he's caught up in the sky.

I asked Albert if that's why so many Indians work on skyscrapers, to get closer to the Spirit.

"Nah," he crowed, then gave his crotch a shake. "We just like showing off our balls. It's an edge we've got on the white man." He paused before adding, "*Most* white men, that is."

I bought him a shot and we set to getting shit-faced.

As the night wore on, Albert asked me about the river, the one I used to guide on when I lived my life back East. I told him all about it. From the foamy white rapids to its less than normal route: an upward, northerly flow. I talked about that river till I missed it like my wife. I think Albert missed it too, in a nostalgic kind of way. It reminded him of his grandfather and the tales he used to share with him when Albert was a child. Stories of the earth's creation, of the mythical warrior twin Child of Water, and of the rivers that gave them life. Just from talking about them, his spirit seemed awoken.

My own couldn't keep up. Later that night, while the Indians swapped stories about their lives back on the rez., I snook off to the bathroom and curled up in a stall, cried an hour straight. I could have

cried longer—maybe longer than any time Hank Williams ever did—
but that drunk-time thought started brewing in my head: I had to call
my wife. The phone was on the wall. I went to it. Dialed the number.
Listened for Patty's voice. Four rings in a robot answered. *This number
has been disconnected*, it said. *Please try again.*

I slammed the phone down then tried another. This time a
woman answered, her "Hello" thick with accent. I recognized the
voice. Mrs. Williams, the kicker's mom. In the background her
husband cursed the tv. Something about a NASCAR race. I hung up
and smacked the wall.

They didn't need to know it was me calling, that I had broken
the judge's orders. It would have only caused them to relive the night
I stumbled into their yard, drunk, dragging a split-up crib. The night I
set that crib on fire. Nothing pretty there. Not when a man stands in
four a.m. night with bright red flames about him like a KKK cross
burning shouting: "You killed my baby! You killed my baby!"

Actually, to tell it truthfully, I shouted: "You killed my
Thomas!" We were going to name him that, after General Thomas
"Stonewall" Jackson. We thought that would be romantic. Or noble.
Or something along those lines, in some traditional Southern way.
Most of the folks we knew from our homes got what we were getting
at. I don't think the Williams' did though. I don't think they got much
of anything, least of which their son. He was probably just a nuisance
to them. A drunken night's mistake. A great leech sucking from their
lives. Name your cliché, it doesn't really matter. Any of them would
fit.

I just wish I could have called *him* that night. Woke him from
his bunker. Asked him why he did it. "How does it feel?" I would
have said. "To be living your life in juvie?" Lucky for the punk, I
passed out on the floor. Albert found me lying there with the phone
still in my hand.

"Who you calling, Kemosabe?" he slurred as he tapped me
slowly awake. All around him shiny trailers from bar lights danced
about the room. It had finally happened, I thought. I had fallen from
a beam and gone to heaven and Albert was St. Peter welcoming me to

the fold. Turns out the night was only over, my purifying complete. That's what Albert said as he lifted me then pointed to the ground.

"See. What did I tell you?"

I followed his finger to the dull pool of puke now puddled around my feet.

"You're free of the poison."

So I was, if only for that moment. Because for the rest of the night I steady hurled my guts. I hurled in the parking lot, out the window of Albert's truck, and still, beside the camper, with my cheek atop the dirt. I hurled so much my ribs began to ache—feel like spears being cast into my side—which stirred up the complaints Patricia made when the baby gave its kicks, and that led to hurling even more.

By the end of it all I was starting to have strange visions. Stonewall Jackson rode up on Little Sorrell and spoke of his war's great horrors and all that was yet to come in God's fight to calm the earth. He said a nightmare had been cast upon the land and that I must take up my sword with valor and that I needed to grow stronger because he too had lost a son and wife but never his heart or head, only part of them.

It was moving, the way he talked. I felt inspired. Not in an Earl-after-reading-a-book kind of way. But in a I-can-be-a-man kind of manner. I was going to tell him about my Patricia back home and how I intended to win her back but then he faded into the sun. Poof! Just up and vanished! I stumbled inside the camper then and played myself at chess.

Alone with all that silence I realized another truth: the poison cannot be emptied. I must take it with me always.

There are three major types of clouds above, and within those types an endless amount of shapes, and when you rise above the norm— the wound up tension that has become our daily grinds—you can see them. You can see them all. Only you have to make it count, the watching of these clouds. For as quick as they form the wind then

74

blows them off, and all that you are left with is a fading, shapeless wisp. An exquisitely painful picture.

Things can leave you that fast. They really, truly can. That's why I study each cloud now as if I'll never see it again.

"How did it happen?" Earl asked one night, out of the blue, while settling before the campfire. "You know, the split with your wife?"

I almost didn't hear him for my head lost in the clouds. Literally, I was staring at some cloud heads that had rolled in on the valley, thinking of that work day, how I had breathed such strong, high vapors, watched them take their shape. I longed for my beam, for the binding of steel and metal. Instead, I floated back down. "That's a rather personal question," I answered. "Don't you think?"

"Not when a man's shared his greatest fears with you a fifth of a mile in the air. *Nothing's* personal after that."

He had a point. Still, how do you relate to another man that you shut down completely in the hours when your wife needed you the most? That when your wife was clinging to you like a first-time beam scaler a thousand feet high and scared out of her mind you failed to talk her down. You could have been there for her, brought her back from that frightened ledge, but instead you stood there frozen; you watched her slip, fall, slowly plummet to the ground, her arms splayed straight, as if expecting you would catch her, her framed like that all the way down until she finally hit the bottom. A hard bottom.

Rock bottom.

I should have walked on clouds then. Walked so gently that my footsteps left no print, no mark upon my wife. If I had it to do over, then I know I surely would, but that doesn't fix what's passed. Doesn't change the fact I'm so ashamed of myself that I couldn't even tell a good friend like Earl the truth about what happened. There was no mention that night of me refusing to speak for days on end, skipping therapy sessions, or quitting my once-loved job. No mention of me mocking my wife's tears—of me becoming a first-rate jerk. I only said, "I drank too much" and left it at that.

75

Of course, Earl didn't buy it. He couldn't have. He's too smart a guy for such fiction. But thankfully he let it go. Maybe he saw the pain still there hiding behind my eyes. I'd felt enough, he must have thought. Why put this man through more?

We talked of some guy named Nietschze instead.

That same night Albert came by to tell us he was leaving, quitting his long-time job for the pursuit of work on water. He said he had found all the answers he could up there in the endless stretch of heavens and that now it was time to go in search of adventures like those savored by his ancestors. He encouraged me to follow. I declined. I figure I've seen about all that land has to offer, can do without the chaos that has seeped into the ground. Give me life with fierce gravity instead.

I do admire his quest though. Every now and then I get a postcard from him from some exotic, far-off place. The last one came from salmon country in Alaska. He said he was making good money there and sending some home to the rez. He said he hunted in his spare time and had killed a giant grizzly. He also said he hoped I had completed my purification process because he hated to see a man as sad as I am but not to worry if I hadn't because for some people the voyage is longer and when they get there the honor great.

He said I was one crazy-ass white dude.

I believe he may be right. I mean, why else would I let Earl talk to me about such tripe as the value of free will? Given what I've been through, there's really no other explanation except that in order to survive I've put all my chips up for grabs. You see, the secret to success as a cloud walker is not caring if you live or die. The second you start contemplating life's value is the second your steps start carrying too much weight, and before you know it—despite the safety gear, the training, or the oath to keep your wits—Splat! You're just another number in the books. A statistic for some other walker to study.

Besides, if you do fall—and God forbid such a thing should happen before Patty takes one of my calls—it's only natural. Like the smart guy said, everything that goes up must come down. Satellites fall from orbit and apples from branches and husbands from their wives' sweet grace. Even angels can fall, if they let themselves.

That's why lately I've tried not to get too down over it all. Things happen, and if you work hard enough, you learn from them. Like when I was seven years old and climbed a giant chestnut tree. I climbed it to the top, fell out, and broke my arm in two places. It's still not the same size as the other one, doesn't really function like it should. I never climbed another tree after that, but on some mornings, when I'm alone on that beam and the sun reveals the world below me in a golden, gracious light, I think to myself: My God! What all I must have missed from that treetop's view. What beauty I could have captured!

In moments like these—epiphanies, Earl calls them—I realize just how low I really am. But one of these days I am going to rise. I am going to rise like the phoenix and set this world ablaze, prove my worth to my wife. That day is not quite here yet, but it will come. It has to come, 'cause not even dreams can end this bad. I just have to remind myself that the past is another place. For now there's the future to hold to—this thing called life to grasp—as I fight to keep my balance.

One Hundred Dozen
(On An Art Installation by Gretchen Jane Mentzer)
Linda Lancione Moyer

In a basement room she's made a huge tree
of grocery sacks. Each sack is crushed,
trampled to a wrinkled sheen,
then set in the mouth of the next
till stack after tight-packed stack form one thick,
undulant trunk to the ceiling—
store logos flaring color like random leaves—
and creep across the floor like surface roots.
The artist swears she has no idea what
she's made, only paid forth months of labor
to birth this form. When asked where she started,
she answers, like God, "In the beginning,"
and you can't blame her. Some things are secret.
This is the turning decade, when what we've begun
becomes unstoppable. All we can do
is take what's on hand, repair, amend,
grow down toward the core and still stretch upward,
salvage from what we've ruined.

Hotel Room Interview
Laurie Blauner

Q: Have you been welcomed here?

A: I found some lost flowers, vegetables, and underwear. The upholstery and I get along. The window is arrogant, trying to leave the same way it came in, and the bed is deeply religious.

Q: How can you be so much like me and yet like everyone else?

A: I fill again and again. I have an imaginary door.

Q: Where would you like to go?

A: To meet in predetermined places. There are rules and I have questions.

Q: Can you describe the outside?

A: Everything I'm not: someone's dream of arrival that has departed.

Q: What keeps you going?

A: I rearrange the curtains and sheets everyday. I wait for her to return
her body to the space that misses her.

Q: How do you feel about glass?

A: It stops me. I see the personality of clouds, uncertain and nothing comes out of them except rain or an occasional plane.

Q: What disturbs you about the sky?

A: It bothers sleeping vagrants, moving their walls around.

Q: What are your conclusions?

A: I'm watching a sleeping man's mouth break open. I'm watching a humorless woman give up her night. I remove them all in their own time and yet I'm never empty.

Burying Bird Dog
Lindsay Wilson

for Cayenne

My ex-girlfriend and I took turns with the shovel
and gathering rocks from the river's shore.

When we finally sat, leaning against each other,
the unleashed wind ran away from between us

into the high-bone grass flushing a murmur
of starlings from the brush. It wasn't the first

time we understood we didn't know how to pray,
but after carrying the heavy stones

to cover her grave, we could feel the phantom
weight of her in our hands.

Memorial Days
Lloyd Milburn

In honor, hats lowered to hearts,
taps brings tears at the appointed time,
while the poet sits alone, nonplussed,
eyes dry the day decreed,

gut storm breaking the day after.

His blue-veined chronometer gland
floats in liquid humours
balanced one day (distilling),
turned toward the moon the next
(pouring). . . .

Veteran tides wash over his shoulder,
its nagging wound aloof to that
arbitrary Gregorian calendar.

The next day, set to Maternal seasons,
his ossicle nerves hear the occasional set of
twenty-one shots accumulating in the clouds
without warning,

whether or not
others still remember.

Kennewick Man
Matthew Campbell Roberts

It is no shame to fail on the last dream
—Jon Turk

Here we go again Kennewick Man.
The paper says you are free now.
It says you traveled through an ice-age,
over scree-fields long before the Columbia
dredged your clay tomb,
and crossed bridges of time
to a world that wasn't new,
a calcified arrow in your hip.
Even after the ice-dams collapsed,
and the Lake Missoula flood
carved desert basins,
before concrete and barges
raised Grand Coulee Dam,
your story lodged in Precambrian sediments.

If you could speak through your shattered jaw
you could let the world know
there's no way back;
the ice-sheets have melted,
the glaciers receded into caves,
the land bridge
submerged beneath the sea.

Let them know I heard your last cry,
traveling rivers
wider than the Nile and Euphrates,
finding your way back
to some lost plain
where all endings and beginnings start.

Evidence
Noel Kalenian

In the tumult of a Friday afternoon
coils of energy too long tightly clamped
yell cross street over traffic
trading jibes for laughs

In the park
boys throw up the ball and
stalk each other at a run
burying one another
with a venom they receive in turn as
the first leaves fall from trees and
birds call from eaves
of buildings imitating castles
drawing up the bridge

Though evening softly bathes our faces as
shoulders lean on iron railings
Though elders wave from stoops
Though seven kids throw dice against the bottom step

Brownstones offer no hints
from concrete courtyards and
stairways descending to
metal doors

Trash cans sit heavy
spilling evidence
of the domestic

Old black women tottering with canes
look aside when I approach
as if something surprising were there
or smile to themselves
acknowledging a secret

Pol Pot
Randy Blythe

Live at zero, address
all are addressed to. End and begin there.

Grow fat on doctrine.

Don't look at blood-smeared leaves.
Enjoy instead, with the farmer's wife,
the beauty in the passing line of neckerchiefs.

Those who question and those who don't
come to themselves at the end of a road.

Think of the unthinkable as your lover
waiting in the thicket outside camp.

After the third accusation,
the standard crime's the most expedient.

With time, treason is an easy ally.

Before you are reported, we are closest friends.

At the end of the boulevard
lined with flag-wavers,
a woman is frying your lungs.

Only when you've pulled off the hen's head can she fly.
I do not care that you have done nothing wrong.

Majesty Muted
Kristin Berkey-Abbott

The poet teaches first year Composition
down the hall from an Astronomy
class. Her students struggle
to turn basic sentences into coherent
paragraphs. Language strips its potential
for majesty as they get back to basics:
subject, verb, direct object.

Over the students' bent heads, the poet hears
whisps of Cosmology from down the hall,
hints of a big bang and dancing around Darwin.
She thinks of that teacher who has seen glimmers
of the mysteries of the universe
and must now use language that lacks
enough words to explain tough concepts to bored students.

The astronomer and the poet, modern mystics, cracked
open by cosmic glories unglimpsed
by most. They return
from the mountaintops
with great news of glad tidings.
They're greeted with the sighs
of those who prefer to have majesty muted.

Time Traffic

Judson Evans

He might have gnawed off his own arm since it was no longer
part of him or climbed the abacus of stacked mirror boxes,
but he rolled up maps of recurrence in a cardboard tube
and caught a cab.

The fare bled into images:
seven ghost written stories,
gargoyles about-faced by sandblasting
stalked a labyrinth of needs exiled in ornament
because the *wayback machine*
has the structure of a sentence.

What was the address, and to whom was it addressed?

Intersection of *Resource*
and *Poverty*.

Mnemonic tree of street names upended by the G.P.S.,
rerouting desire — closed exits, palaces of flesh
gone to flea market—, the city's love song of static
through news and crackling
intercom: back after break-up, teen idols *Earth* and *Sky* —
and window displays flushed out like aquariums,
while stagnant transmissions
hung between skyscrapers,
drift nets draping bridges.
In back of the cab, head lolling, tattooed in neon,
the yellow glow of the traffic light

suffused his face. Granary besotted with grain, x-ray
as passport. Do we love what is *good*
or merely what is over?

Aubade with a Panic of Hearts
Traci Brimhall

When you blindfold me, I hear an owl hunting
        outside our window, hear the heartbeats
    of mice skittering between the walls.

You lie on me, play dead. You want to prove
        I can't leave you. When I can't breathe,
    you peel dead skin from my lips and say,

Hold still. I want to tell you something.
        You say there's snow on the magnolias,
    and I know you've been dreaming

about her again. I won't forgive you
        even if you kiss me, even if you pin
    my neck to the bed and kiss me.

A mouse bruxes behind the baseboards, but its pulse
        spikes when it hears your iron voice.
    After you set the traps, you pull back the sheets

to marvel at my marked skin. Why won't you
        ever close the curtains? I can see wilted violets
    in the window boxes and birches unscrolling.

We must forgive each other, or pity each other,
        or set fire to the house. Untie me. I need
    to stop the panic of hearts behind the wallpaper.

Can't you hear it? The blood parade in the sheetrock.

The owl's golden eyes opening. When I call your name like a question into the darkness, the darkness answers.

Prayer to Delay the Apocalypse

Angels, give us this day. Set down your plagues,
    and forgive us this night. I've lifted a candle to see
        who I've been making love to and examined his body

for the first signs of terror. Whoever you are, wake up.
    Tell me heaven will be like Venice—dirty, beautiful
        and sinking. Tell me the walls of every paradise fall,

that there are riots in the city of peace. Promise me
    I will die of love. Promise me we take our suffering
        with us, the scratches we crewel down each other's

backs as we rush into joy. Take the ghosts first,
    they have gone wild with grief. Let the apostles pull up
        their nets. Keelhaul the archangels, make seraphs kiss

the sharks, but do not call me unto you. Do not spare me
    gunshots outside my window. Do not spare me the man
        who touched my neck on the train to St. Petersburg

when he thought I was asleep. The devil has been up all night
    and is sleeping it off in the basement. Let him rest awhile.
        Let us continue wandering in these perishable machines

made of dirt and music. The saguaros swell with rain.
    Hallelujah. The mysteceti's heart is big enough to crawl
        through and it sings for no reason, hallelujah. Praise

for young seahorses growing in their fathers' bodies.
    Praise for the avocados clinging to the trees as dusk steals
        the sky. I will hold on to the night like a girl with wet hair.

I will put my fingers into bullet holes in the opera house. Do not
    destroy this. Gone would be Goya, Paris and the Marinsky ballet.
        Gone the glaciers and Great Barrier Reef. Gone the cave

paintings where humans first learned we must love
    what we kill. My dear God, my darling Torquemada,
        the first and the last and the everlasting, you already know

how this will end, how as a child I heard *Talitha cum*
    and woke standing over my father, saw the fire
        burning next to him. I nestled into the curve of him

and pretended to sleep so he would take me back to bed,
    bear me like a bowl brimming with water, like an angel
        carry me to the end of the world and lay me down.

The Supposed Kingdom
Judson Simmons

1.

Waking, again, I find myself
lost amongst the shade
of another overcast morning.

My feet and hands, legs
and spine are heavy
with wear, unable to function.

Something catches my eye:
a spider web held at its corners
by ceiling and wall.

Spread like a tapestry, a maze
of silken threads—I leave behind
my body to inherit dust

and dirt, letting my mind carry
towards this thin net, finding myself
caught like a curious fly.

2.

I'm tired, yet my eyes
can rest no more. It seems
that every night is an eternal loop,

an album left on repeat—
playing to an empty room.

Next to me, you are sleeping. Lost
in a somewhere far from here;
you don't notice as I slip
to my feet from beneath
the covers—the floor is cold
to the touch, with each step
the floorboards creak
like an aching back.

The night must understand
how I feel, the anxiety
of never being at rest: something,
car or creature, always moving.
The earth keeps moving…

3.

Like a hanged man,
the spider dangles. Slowly
it climbs the noose
towards a repenting fly.

God is like that—a fly
caught in the sticky bind
of the spider, our mind.

We hold God close,
feast upon His existence
as the world keeps watching.

4.

I look back towards
the window; you are there,
I know, still fixed
to a web of sleep.

An early fog settles
on our lawn. I slip
into a darkness,
the supposed kingdom
of my body—a fragile home

to resign every emotion,
every movement.

To Ward Off Thefts of Memory
Christine Hope Starr

The missing sometimes happens when I consider the 1,200 miles between North Carolina and Nebraska. Or, it happens when I sample a well-aged cheddar wedge he offered, a trapezoid of pineapple, or lick the salt off a baked potato skin, when I break apart clods of dirt with my hands or when I breathe a rose that is more fruity than floral. Such sensory pleasures seasoned our family life; mostly it was duck and cover, and wait for the storm of Dad to pass over. But, buried as he was in overwork and fury, I mined for him and loved him for the ore of his singular human life. I call when I miss him or when he might miss me.

"I was thinking of you," I say. "I was telling a story. You'd laugh to hear me."

"Oh?"

"I got it from you. The storytelling. And the story."

He is quiet and I know he is breathing past the bloom of a knot in his throat. My fearsome father weeps in recent years, brimming it seems with melancholy and perhaps the recognition that the time to make many things right strode past when he was watching stocks or making his name matter or maintaining the hard, sharp line of discipline. His awareness of what he's lost seems to mount as his riches recede. I want him to be at peace with his choices—because my peace partially depends on it.

"I suppose it's because I bought a Napoleon Torte for Allie's birthday."

"Oh, yah," he sighs. "Those are something."

"A *small* one!"

"Sure. They're not cheap."

"I got thinking about that other torte."

"Sure." He knows why. The story of the torte is a secret handshake for us.

Napoleon Torte from the Lithuanian Bakery in Omaha brags sweet strata of butter, apricot, and pastry, the texture and taste of which linger years after you tease it onto a fork and raise the layers to your lips. It's the sort of dessert that calls to mind the person with whom you ate it, the occasion when you dared your diet with it, or the host generous enough to spend the cash so you could partake without guilt or expense.

When Dad brought a massive sweet wheel home one nearly spring Saturday, squeezed sideways into a grocery bag laid flat, I had never seen a version of the torte that big. On a few special occasions, we'd had one at home perhaps nine inches across. This devil must have been a good 15 to 18 inches in diameter. It weighed as heavy as the several pounds of butter it contained. But when your oldest daughter becomes engaged, you splurge if you can. It's allowed, even expected.

Through the door, past the pantry, the VIP torte made its way in Dad's arms. My sister Kathy understood and appreciated the carriage, the investment in dessert for her party. Her fiancé, Mark, registered it in his quiet way, still fancying my sister sweeter.

"Open the fridge," Dad said, balancing the torte and nodding at me.

We could both see it wouldn't fit. The shelves were brimming with other party foods and the usual extensive contents of my parents' well-stocked refrigerator. Dad didn't like surprises on party days. I didn't like his not liking them.

"Cripes! What are we gonna do with it?" He looked desperate for only a moment. "Open the garage door," he commanded and stepped out, laying his burden to rest on the waiting expanse of his cherished and rarely driven import. The Daimler. Parked in the cool garage, the gray hood of it stretched long and level. As the evening wore on, it would only get cooler.

We all set to work finalizing everything for guests. The vacuum roared. And so did Dad now and then. But we remained in good

99

spirits, anticipating a bright and polite cadre of college friends of theirs to celebrate their upcoming June wedding. The only setback was a dearth of beer. Dad hadn't considered that such young guests weren't the sorts to order up mixed drinks like his usual corporate partygoers. Mark offered to run and returned just before the bash with a couple of cases of mid-priced beer to seed in ice we'd harvested from the upstairs and downstairs freezers. Mark was almost giddy. He had taken Dad up on an offer to drive the Daimler on this short errand. It drove like a dream, he reported. And everyone stared, just as he'd said they would and, yes, Mark had managed the right-hand driver's side without too much trouble. I could tell that Kathy was proud of the trust our father had placed in her man.

The young couples began to arrive and Kathy and Mark enjoyed showing them around the home my parents expertly entertained in. Some played pool in the basement. Others relaxed beneath the palm and ficus trees that sheltered the indoor pool, tended by a service that came several times a year. They dined all over the house: at our two curved black Formica bars, at the rattan table, and from their laps. Laughter rang in all the rooms. Dad began circulating among the guests to assess their readiness for dessert, and to build the anticipation that he would satisfy when he brought forth a treat he was sure none of them had experienced.

It was time. I followed him up to the garage and opened the door ceremoniously. He froze, bearing a puzzled expression, then turned back toward the kitchen, glancing over the long custom countertops his youngest brother, a cabinetmaker, had fashioned in Northern Minnesota and trucked to Nebraska for my 4'11" mother.

"What the hell? Eileen!" he bellowed.

Mom appeared quickly, her face saying, don't yell and ruin things.

"What did you do with the torte?"

"I didn't do anything with it."

"Well, it isn't there." He gestured to the garage as if that proved she'd done it.

They went together and peered from the doorway, then stepped out and walked all around the car. Nothing. The wheels in Dad's head were turning. He paced off the steps to the outer door of the garage. Sure enough, it was unlocked.

"Someone stole the damned torte!" he announced.

By then, Kathy had joined them and was trying to reassure Dad, against all odds, that everything would be fine.

It was not fine. In our nice neighborhood, it was almost too much to bear. But Dad, never one to shirk responsibility as a party host, stepped into the house, captured everyone's attention, and shared the painful news. No dessert. He savored at least sharing its impressive girth, an expanse so great that it couldn't be housed in the family fridge. Two dozen sympathetic faces looked on, shaking their heads collectively like bobble-head dogs. A thief, it was hard to even say it, must have discovered it on the hood of the Daimler and carried it off, he finished.

It was Mark who first registered the words "hood of the Daimler." Then asked, not wanting to ask, "When did you put the torte on the Daimler? And was it..." This was the hardest part. "...in a brown paper grocery sack?"

Nobody breathed. Dad looked like he might erupt. "My God, man! Do you mean you drove off with it?"

The torte of course had been on the left side of the Daimler, closest to the kitchen door. Mark, the overwhelmed, first-time driver of a fine, foreign automobile had looked over the hood on the right side as he got his bearings, figured out the unusual positions of the controls, looked over his shoulder to carefully back out. Everything was so new. He wanted to be so careful.

Kathy bowed her head, mortified.

The first brave soul to answer in Mark's place was another man. "I saw a paper bag in the road on my way here. I straddled it. I didn't know what was inside and didn't want to take a chance on running over it. You know, and damage my car." With that, a collective firing of synapses ignited in our guests' brains, each exclaiming about *their* respective encounters with *the bag* and their oft-repeated decision to straddle the potentially dangerous object. Finally, one offered that it was only about a block away, just after the turn onto the street that adjoined my parents' own Sunshine Boulevard.

101

Did we dare collect the body? Like a tribe of hunters, we streamed out the front door with Mark in the lead. As soon as we made it a half block down our hill, we could all see it, the brown bag taut but fluttering beneath the glow of the streetlight. Mark knelt beside it, afraid to look, but resolute. He grasped the lip of the bag and turned it. We heard the grate of loose gravel underneath. He raised it slightly and we could hear his incredulous laugh as he spoke. "My God, it's whole. It's perfect."

"It's such a great story," I say to Dad.

"Yah...and when we found it all eaten by those dogs," he says.

What dogs? There were definitely no dogs. "Dad?" I say it like the line went dead. "What was so amazing was that it was untouched. You know?" And I wait in the alarm and writhing of silence for his answer.

"Sure. That's right. I'm thinking of something else."

A typical scenario with my school-age daughters plays out at least a couple of times a week now. It goes like this: one of them starts reeling out a *bit*, like a movie trailer. The other one almost immediately recognizes a fragment and joins in. They are laughing, adding details by the half-minute. I want to join in, and am madly scrambling to remember where any of the fragments came from. Was this part of a real event in our lives, a show they saw with me, a show they only told me about, a funny remembrance only *they* share? I paddle in my mental pool, glancing left and right, and most commonly find I'm alone there. Finally, I surrender and ask them to "name that bit." It is always painful to me when they provide the context and it is well known to me. Why can't I pick out the random strands of their stories anymore? Why can't I riff with them? Where do all our anecdotes go, the ones so carefully stacked for so long at the front of my brain?

Just a few weeks ago, my hands forgot their left- and right-handedness as I looked out my picture window in the living room. The landing of a cardinal beside his mate in the junipers helped my sense of right and left click into place again—*Oh, she's to the left of him*, I thought. East and West are set by the relative position of the sun to our left or right, and we sometimes lose our corporeal bearings for no apparent reason. I often exit stores, especially those that open onto large parking lots, having no idea which way to turn to find my parked car. Wait, I tell myself. Wait. And there is an almost imperceptible flutter in my brain as the world rights itself.

My new friend, Mary, shared a story with me during our weekly phone call.

"I guess I left it on the roof of my car," she said. "I can't believe he brought it to me. A mile from home it fell off…"

The memory wheel had begun to turn toward torte with those words of hers, but before I began to tell my story, I listened to hers. As it unfolded, I pictured Mary's hero standing at her door, nodding over his shoulder to acknowledge the gravel Indiana road behind him, the one that carried her away from her airborne wallet and drew him to that same road-kill billfold, its leather surface muddy, scuffed from tumbling. At 88, a woman needs both hands to get in the car. The pocketbook had lain waiting on top, then taken flight when she accelerated.

"And the money was still inside," she said. "Over a hundred dollars."

"How about that," I said.

"I told him to take the money. He earned it."

"That's very kind of you."

"He wouldn't have it!" she shot back with delight.

I pictured the stranger passing this pop quiz of character, a chivalrous man, perhaps one of the last ones left in the South, since the tiptoe of Indiana is considered the South by regional consensus as locals say it is more Kentucky than Indiana there. I picture Mary, the proud matriarch of a sprawling, full-grown family of eight children, collecting an anecdote with which to inoculate her great-grandsons against cynicism, to stretch their not-yet-finished characters to this measure of a man who wouldn't take advantage of an old woman even in hard times.

"Well, he was decent," I finally said. "He was doing the right thing."

"I finally got him to accept forty dollars. He seemed pleased with that."

Happily, our conversation never veers in the direction of her age. Aren't we all quick to frame stumbles in our elder friends and relatives as by-products of aging? Instead, I tell about the time I cruised behind a midsize sedan that had a torpedo of zucchini on top. Three blocks and a sharp corner and it never budged. Better than that was the woman in the SUV. I followed her from my daughter's high school, certain she had one of those decals on her bumper that makes people do a double take. The coffee cup looked terribly realistic. But wait. At the next red light, I jammed my van into park and jumped out. It took only an instant to lunge, grab the cup, and appear at the driver's-side door. The automatic window sailed down, the woman inside said thanks and snagged the cup. As I leapt back into my own car, the light changed. This is all a deftly slanted ramp to carry Mary to the torte story, a tale that makes her laugh and exclaim.

Telling her is what stirred up the longing to talk to Dad. Now, we are quiet on the phone, both stalled by his gaffe.

"I love you," I say to him.

"I love you too, Hon."

"I should get going here," I say, not actually needing to do anything.

"I'm glad you called."

Like a mountain range, he is supposed to be my reference point for all the stories of our family, forever. Was this slip of his an errant zucchini, a forgotten wallet, a hastily misplaced morning coffee, or the murmurings of a hurricane about to tear away the oral storehouse I've come to rely on, hauling out tape recorders recently, anticipating the day when he is gone, a very far-off day?

I confess I'm not interested in the pathos of another early onset of Alzheimer's account, as anguished and legitimate as they are, even if my own father could be its next victim. It is memory itself that compels me, where it resides, what enlivens it, what extinguishes it, how we take it for granted, how we judge people expertly and inexpertly in command of it, what catalyzes our wariness around others' forgetfulness and vigilance regarding our own.

We are all so busy inside and out. It is a wonder we keep anything straight. I press the end button and consider how I was surprised decades ago by Dad's seamless movement between the demands of corporate life and the quiet work of landscaping at home. It felt like a secret he kept. Did members of the board of Mutual of Omaha know how he cupped dozens of fledgling annuals in his hands the evening after a hard-won victory at the company or a long day slogging through meetings? Had any of them ever guessed he could unload boulders and plant them like trees in the berms he groomed around our home?

They knew of at least one unhidden talent. He was in demand at company functions because of his unrivaled talent at storytelling; he was the de facto master of ceremonies when he was in attendance. Reeling the conferees in and rolling the stories out came easily to him. The ease impressed people as much as the tales did, for there is a certain envy that attends listening to a gifted storyteller—the command of myriad details, the timing, the accents and dialects he could pluck from space impressed everyone. An exceptionally competent businessman who kept them rolling in the aisles was great for morale and sales. You couldn't pay for such skills.

It hadn't occurred to me that any of him would leave before he did. I make a note to ask his wife if she's noticed any changes in his memory, but in three calls, I don't ask her. I won't. He lives far from the triggers now: the people, the places, the times, and the urgings to tell his stories. No one in North Carolina challenges those muscles. Of course they are flabby.

My long-ago neighbor, Rose, in the apartment beside mine when I was an undergraduate living in Lincoln's college ghetto, used to share the same half dozen stories with me. She lived alone with the dullest rhythm to her day and no way to discriminate between days. Most weeks, she told her stories over a Corelle plate layered with oatmeal cookies, a ritual I surmise she was certain I looked forward to as much as she did. She couldn't see the roaches skittering across the plate when she offered them to me. Her elderly daughter hadn't gotten her in to have her eyes checked, as outings with Rose were dependent on her descending the porch stairs. The stairs might as well have been a ski slope. Too, her heavy curtains were often drawn to save on heat, creating a dim atmosphere in which I loudly carried on my end of our visits so she could hear me better. When she raised the plate with her lined hand, I politely drew a cookie or two from it and tried to think brown sugar thoughts as I munched them.

Why didn't I just jump and cry, "Whoa, Rose, roaches!" After those we know reach a certain age, we attribute most anomalous events to decrepitude. *Poor thing. She doesn't know any better. I don't want to hurt her feelings.*

All these years later, I'm mad at myself for letting Rose serve me those cookies. Those roaches were likely crawling over *all* her meals. I haven't thought about that in years. I forgot. So, I tell myself, it is good if moderately embarrassing to call Dad on his error, to treat it like the fluke it might well have been, a moment of inattention, or an organic and trivial misfiring of brain synapses like my parking lot fogs, trouble seeing through the ripples the stone makes in the clear surface of the lake, not a marker I'll return to in a year or two to recall when *it* began.

Which of Dad's stories are memories, and which are memorized? There's a difference.

At 45, I volunteered to join a troupe of amateur actors in a dinner play during a vacation stay in North Carolina (actor is too lofty a moniker for what I brought to the venture). I agreed to it only because everything in my life was in disarray. It made twisted sense to do something I thought I couldn't do. I was in the opening moves of getting a divorce after 20 years and trying to imagine me as something more and less than I'd ever been. For a week, I donned a blond wig and belted out semi-humorous lines in a faux southern accent, bringing *Southern Fried Murder* to a forgiving and appreciative local crowd. My dress was low cut. I had a temporary tattoo above my breast. Several men approached me to ask if I was really like Stump, my character, in real life. "No," I told these creepers (er, enthusiastic fans), "I'm not." But, before the opening, I had to memorize 150

106

lines and the cue lines of other actors that would elicit mine. I copied them carefully onto index cards. I held the weighty deck and shook my head. No way. Then I heard the echo of my grandmother's voice at 80-something reciting a lengthy poem from her childhood with the drama and flare of a woman younger than I was then. In a few short days, we went off book (as they say in theater when you are no longer allowed to carry your script with you) and I managed. We all found ways to draw the words from those scripts into our own heads and mouths as if we'd thought them up. Amazing. A few years later, I can't call up even one line.

I spent five excruciating weeks in college-level calculus one summer.

Even earned an A+. All gone.

In nine years with a dance studio, I memorized dozens of steps.

I can see myself on stage and off as if in a film, remember smells, sounds, and anguish.

My arms, legs, and body can't recount any of the moves.

In fact, memorizing and memory seem utterly unrelated to me, despite their common stem. Memories form and arrange themselves in my mind with a somewhat natural ease as I enjoy my time on the planet. They are imperfect, even porous, but accumulate and compound for the most part without my special effort. I don't strive to remember what happens to me. Nobody has to compel me to take remembrances down on index cards and rehearse them. Even so, my memory is apparently more acute or at least better organized for later access than my four siblings', more like Dad's I want to say.

When my mom turned 70, my two brothers, two sisters, and I chose to celebrate her milestone birthday with a party. I was the night's designated speaker and put together a written walk through her decades. Close in age as we all are, my siblings were stunned at the things I remembered. They were able to corroborate those memories, as was Mom, but their capacity to beckon them was different than mine. My brain seems to have an elaborate warehouse of memories large and small that I can rifle through to my own pleasure and the delight of listeners.

The first time I lost a previously cherished memory, in whole or in part, it was moderately distressing, just as was the realization after my parents' divorce that many stories of our growing up would leak away, for some memories are held cooperatively. Mom might begin, "You were five and I think Teresa was very sick…" Dad interjects, "Yes…that was when we took her to the hospital because you had the flu too," which causes Mom to say, "That's right. And the neighbors had to take Mike to school for a week…" at which point Dad says, "He liked it so much he didn't want us to take him after that." And on it goes with one and then the other smiling and remarking how they'd forgotten that. Our family history is co-owned, and upon my parents' divorce, I lost the chance to ever take such treasured side trips again.

We all use triggers to remember and I wonder whether it really *is* a natural part of aging to forget or whether it is strictly the recession of triggers that hampers our recall. None of this explains my parking lot disconnects. That's a mystery I still lack the knowledge to solve. And, it creates in me a nagging feeling that I am *weak* in that area and may be an Alzheimer time bomb waiting to blow. So much like Dad, I remind myself. And is the storytelling acumen we share genetic, an organic prize to be rescinded in old age, or is it memetic?

Before I step into Target, I look around to identify landmarks that will guide me without hesitation to my car. But, when I'm done shopping, when I exit with my bag of things I don't really *need*, the familiar strangeness envelops me anyway. Wait, I say. Wait.

Neighborhood Watch
Raegen Pietrucha

As your hands pass over the circle,
your time should guarantee
separation; yet here I stand,

years later, in the cul-de-sac
with my childhood house.
You mark three in the morning

and 29 years for me.
There haven't been ghosts
in the graveyard here for years.

I don't know if these new children
have ever played our old games.
I don't know what they have to fear

from long nights in this ritzy subdivision –
the kind without streetlights,
because the really rich

are partitioned; a child could fall
asleep outside on a lawn chair and wake up
suffering nothing

but a few bug bites and the cold.
Fate has made me their teacher,
though they often slump at their desks,

counting down your ticks, playing
with gadgets that hadn't yet been invented
when I was them. Truth is, I can't relate;

there's no way
I can know what they think,
let alone what they fear.

Unless it's what I feared,
which was inside this house.

Seeing Stars

As a child   I learned this trick

pressed fingertips   to closed eyelids

                                        made the stars appear

When I opened my eyes

                        blurred

                                        darkness

                Who's there

I couldn't speak what I feared most   believed speaking made *real*

                summoned things into being again

Third-grade amnesiac

                        late-night TV's snowy stars sizzling

                                        hoping light

would scare anything waiting

                        in darkness
                                    to prey

*

Learning the right kind of kiss

            the blazing in my chest

                        a whole universe I could spin

                                    hold in like my breath

    until my dizzy head   lovedrunk   overwrote the past

                                    humming in my skull

But as swiftly as the moon across the sky

                each *he* saw *me*

                gaped at the trails my stars had marked me with

                            and fled

*

No wonder no boy will love you

                Look at you

                            You don't listen he said

Then Father's knuckly yanks raked the lengths of my hair

                          fingers treading neck   nails puncturing flesh

But no matter how bright

                        stars are always quiet

       couldn't save me

                                   from numb

reminded me to cloak my words

                                  left me dumb

*

There's nothing extraordinary

                 about housing stars

silenced tragedies adorning

the always engulfing night

To think people strive

to learn their names

care about naming
them

always waiting for their stupid   distant light to reach

as if
that touch is
kind

Just speaking of them sets them in
their searing motion

and from there   no escape

from their twisted
elliptical fates

Listen

I'm carving out a new star

I create

        as easily as I say the words

*

I search for some hero

    some Orion without a loosed belt

        who will sing the lullaby

           that can put me to sleep

        who can sing the song

           that brings me back to dream

But can *he* exist

        without all those rivets of stars

    Who's there

        still waiting

           for the night

               to rise

Tony: Love Poem
Joanna Rose

You and I walk the dogs in the evening
through meadows where there are yellow birds
in blackberry thickets, a steel scented breeze
from a far glacier and along the highway a train
pulled away by its own whistle,

The tall grass paths criss-cross wide fields,
go all the way to the river, beyond trees in green haze,
farther than I have ever gone.

Requiem
Dorothy Stroud

Services attended by:
weeping children,
dying flowers,
somber dirges for
month-long hours,
long, black ribbons,
joyless laughter,
gray butterflies
came struggling after.

Mourners quiet
in a helpless way.
A favorite word
has died today.

The Albigensian

James B. Nicola

I lie in the south of France.
The grass roots pierce and itch.
When I was slain they neglected the pinewood box.
And the bed they laid me in is yet unmarked.
And since no one living mourned
I have passed a restive time
unable to sleep and not really awake.
But I know where I lie
which is in the south of France.

And I have been able to travel.
I've been to Siberia, Armenia,
Cambodia, South America, Germany, Africa,
and once or twice to a barbed-wired place
under a flag of America
where I've seen the unimaginable and learned
how lucky I am to have lived
where the roots hurt only a little
and to know where I lie which is in the south of France.

Hounds from Hell
Jerome Long

Every morning, punctual,
with the alarm clock's first ring,
begins their incessant baying.
My mother, bless her soul,
calls me her favorite names:
sluggard, ne'er-do-well,
nail biter, infidel. Her harrowing
voice a factory whistle
calling every offence to work.
Next, dear father howls
in my ear: get up, get out
of bed, another day
of defeat and shame awaits
you, bonnie lad. I seem to hear
a choir of nuns singing a matins song:
What will you ever do
to make up for the wrongs
you've done? The good Lord
our Savior died for the crummy
likes of you. Despair. Despair.
By the time I pull myself out of bed
the hounds are already at my head.

Uniform
James Valvis

The sound a rusty chain link fence makes
when the bully pushes you into it
is like a snake striking in anger
and when the punch twists in your guts
decapitating your breath
you look up into the bully's blue eyes
and apologize for what you did wrong
even if you don't know what that is

On your knees now you hear the fence
rattling its loose metal against poles
as the bully leaves you gasping
like someone praying
and at home your uniform shirt
is spotted with nose blood in front
and grilled with rusty X's on the back
your pants are shredded at the knees

It's September and this school uniform
was supposed to last until June
and when your father sees it destroyed
he screams uniforms aren't cheap
money doesn't grow on trees
who do you think I am? Rockerfella?
as the belt is slowly peeled from his waist
and you get more of what you deserve

In Uncertain Light
Daniel Harrington

Stumbling over river stones with uncertain steps
I catch you there, on the edge
Your faintest movement an echo
Fading into softness.

The musk of cottonwood on river-moistened air
Pulls me into the breeze.
Amid the glowing stones of twilight.
Your faintest form there and gone.

The river laps the fading shore.
The sky wears a leaded mask.
Each stumble loosens hollow rocks.
Soft taps of rain begin their gentle reminder.

You skip across a riffle
You dance through shifting leaves
The trace of you a flicker in my periphery
But twilight ghost, I know you.

I have walked in uncertain light,
And I know that I am alone.

The Vacuum
D. Lifland

I was once a black hole.
Always taking more than I gave.
Never going out of my way.
Always looking for the payback.
Imposing my will on others.
Demanding love —
no questions asked.

You can't see my mangled hands,
nor my acid-dipped fingers,
but Mother,
Father,
I'm close to you.
I'm coming home with a heart
that's a suitcase
filled with presents.

Vanishings
Amy Schutzer

The Rogue River churns through
a narrow canyon, the ravens can't
be heard as they fly their rounds.
I know they are there. Death too flourishes
outside this pebbled bend where October glazes
the vine maples. Why should this river remember
the springs where it first pitched out from the earth?
Look around: the world is made to erode
and slip into another state
of further decay—it is not without its beauty:
the volcanic rock is pocked and sky pools
in the slight divots of captured water,
that is to say, I am looking down.
The river doesn't hold anything,
not its beginning, not its end.

Lumber
Bryan C. Brunton

My sisters and I are stacked evenly.
Five thick horizontal planks that stretch too far to see,
wearing finely penciled lines and angles.
Hickory or holly.
I can almost smell us.

A power saw descends and makes quick work of my sisters.
Sliced smoothly and for all their beauty
and outward seeming strength
with no effort.
The high whine of the blade turns to me.

At first it bites but then meeting more resistance,
it cracks and shatters.
I rejoice and knowingly peer close to admire
the barely scored tightness of my grain,
my stiff cable-like filaments.

I lift my eye to the surrounding slaughter –
there is nothing to be done for my sisters,
now cut into perverse arches, sleek and ready for assembly.
If only I had been placed on top and the tool had come first for me.
Pliable and weak they had not been properly hardened.

This thought invades my length,
down my sides I perceive the knobby, warped bigotry of it.
That wrenching shame is then challenged by
seeing the discarded, smoking shell of the power tool
and knowing it to be my father.

Redwood
Christina Lloyd

There's an emergency tonight-
the tree's about to topple over,
about to smash the house into bits
and she wants to chop it down.

Last week the maid put a dead mouse
on her bed, some voodoo to spite her
and she urged me to call the priest
for purification, not once thinking

of the culprit poodle bringing back
its morbid boon from the geraniums,
nasturtiums fumbling over themselves,
the only brightness in this place.

Next week the neighbors, Homeland
Security, might bulldoze her living room.
For now I tell her to leave the tree alone,
that there is time till its roots lose their grip.

A Man Like My Father
Pamela Gullard

My father, Coryell Hintikka, the renowned sociologist, liked striding across the cherry blossom-scented UW campus in his black greatcoat. With his big shoulders and dark-brown, wavy hair, he looked like Voltaire ushering in the Enlightenment, according to one of his eager teaching assistants. Skinny freshmen in new slickers sometimes waved shyly at the handsome man featured on the cover of their Welcome Huskies packets. The brightest graduate students caught up with him, hoping to ask a question or two. They had studied his 1972 classic *The Sociology of Cities*, wherein he predicted the middle-class flight back to the inner cities. When I was young, I wondered why *inner city* didn't refer to a giant, collective soul. But I kept this thought—and most others—from my father.

At home, he was an intellectual brute, a philanderer, a soul crusher. My mother and I kept this quiet. Almost until the very end, my mother loved walking through Seattle on her famous husband's arm. She was slender, pale, her hair twisted high so blond strands crossed her brow in the wet breeze. On campus, my parents were enviously called The Couple. At home, my father shamed my mother into reading *The New York Times*, *The Atlantic*, *The Economist*, then browbeat her when she forgot senators' names or details of the Superfund. Fighting tears, she clung to the romance of the idea that my father had rescued her from an unimportant life.

She told me that she was just 19 when he plucked her from behind the counter of her family's block-long deli with 18 tables in Ballard, Seattle's Scandinavian district. Flirting with her, my father casually put his large hand over one of the hearts carved into the woodwork by the cash register, and she was smitten.

127

Years later, on a cold October evening in 1990, my parents gave an elaborate dinner party to celebrate some honor the editors of *Sociology Today* had bestowed on my father. My mother and I spent two weeks planning and cooking. One of my father's guests was his girlfriend, Jeanne, a professor of French literature with a hawk nose, swinging hair, and an acid tongue. For the first time, he had brought the enemy into our home fortress. Jeanne's undeniable presence was against my parents' unspoken agreement.

While my mother served tender meatballs simmered in milk with a flat potato bread called lefse, my father, sitting at the head of the long table next to me, reached under the tablecloth and patted Jeanne's thigh. My mother, standing by the sideboard, froze, squeezed her eyes shut.

Father was knowingly, cunningly challenging her existence. I think he just wanted to see how far he could push her.

Strangely, in those days I thought of my cerebral father as a farmer on a tractor with a huge windshield (did tractors have windshields?). My mother and I—and actually his girlfriends and students too—were the gnats that happened to strike the glass. Occasionally he would deliberately veer into one of us, but usually he had his sights on a distant horizon, a darkly setting sun that pulled him forward.

My mother jumped off the Aurora Bridge the morning after the party. In mid-air, she must have had a wonderful view of the hills of her old neighborhood. I pictured her chaotic perspective as she tumbled. For weeks after the funeral, my cheeks ached and I couldn't speak, my eyes turned cold, my ears were packed with cotton. I was 17.

My father dramatically played the haunted genius who had been all too human and now was sorry, sorry, sorry. His friends—a group of men who joined the faculty about the same time he did—came to our house and sat with him. I put the casseroles their wives made in our huge old refrigerator. My father, wearing socks and a sweatshirt with baggy corduroys, put his head in his hands at the long table and told his friends that he took full responsibility. He seemed to have sponged up my mother's death and left none for me.

To demonstrate his profound sense of guilt, my father took on a huge teaching load, many more classes than any full professor in the history of the sociology department. His friends told him how brave he was.

Two months after my mother's death, I cooked his morning egg too hard. He held onto the plate and sent it flying into the sink, saying it tasted like a poached baseball and that I cooked like I thought, carelessly and with no finesse.

My jaws ached. "Leave me alone," I said. "I'm mourning my mother."

My father wore the rumpled plaid shirt and red tie he would teach in. "All the more reason to pay attention. You don't want to go down in sloppiness."

"Go down where?" I asked. "Give specifics." His line. Did he think I was my mother? She'd cry. Not me. I had dreamed the night before that someone dropped me from a great height, and my head cracked open on the sidewalk. In the dream, I sat up and thought calmly, *I wonder if I'm dead?* If my mother had miraculously hit land, would she have broken something but still breathed?

My father snorted. There was a pause. He put the empty plate on the table, looked at it. He said gently, "Go down to hell, little girl." He glanced up at me. "She was the love of my life," he said. "So I had to make her pay." He rubbed the corner of his mouth with one finger. "I knew it at the time. I just couldn't stop." His face was damp.

"You could've stopped," I said. She was gone.

"I could have." He cried. I let him fold me against his chest for a minute. Then he went to class.

I stood in the kitchen, numbed by the kitchen towels folded on the counter by the sink, by the salt and pepper shakers shaped like bluebirds that my father disdained as kitsch, by the clean coffee spoons up-ended in a red glass the way my mother's Norwegian family always did. I turned to break the hold of the kitchen.

I thought this conversation with my father would soften things between us, but within days he seemed to forget it ever occurred. If anything, he became even more inexplicably furious. He criticized the black outfits I wore to Roosevelt Public High School as "trite weeds," asked me why I let my mother's house get so dirty, and started pawing through my backpack to find graded papers—I wrote like a zombie, but the grades were sometimes good. In the margins he scrawled "fatuous" or "you've got to be kidding me." I began staying out late with my boyfriend, An Sung, who avoided my father. My father couldn't bear to be avoided. Once, at midnight, he locked me out. My house keys were mysteriously gone from my backpack. I jimmied the bathroom window and slid in over the radiator. My father told me the next morning that I needed to understand the consequences of sneaking around and wasting my potential. He was talking about *my* sneaking?

Finally, early one September night, I came home to a dark house. My father seemed gone, and I couldn't get in. He knew I was taking my test for college the next morning. Was he inside with his old girlfriend, Jeanne? Was he deliberately ruining my future? Rain battered the porch overhang. Did some ancient gripe he had against the universe well up, making him want to defeat someone, me, just because he could?

At the time I didn't wonder about his motives or think about anything. I pounded on the front door of our porch. No answer. I went to the side door at the kitchen. The bathroom window. All locked. How could he? I screamed so the neighbors could hear, "Open up! I'm your *daughter*, you bastard!" Nothing.

I took the little path back to the street and walked for an hour in the rain to An's room above the Pike Place Market. An was 28, a ceramicist who lived in Seattle during summers and some winter weekends. A gallery in the Post Alley showed his bulbous vases and huge plates in strong, layered colors—chartreuse and shades of violet. When not in Seattle, An lived in Santa Barbara, where he made new work. My father knew none of this.

130

I asked An if I could go home with him to California on the coastal train on Monday. He leaned on the over-painted door jamb, his shiny hair that I loved brushing his shoulder. "Yes," he said, kissing me on the forehead. He held me away and looked in my face. "You're freezing. Let me run the water hot in the shower."

I lived in An's large, second-story apartment near the beach and got a job at Trondheim Sandwich and Pastries. The work suited me. I liked slicing off chunks of liverwurst and labeling the wooden markers naming the cheeses. I loved the smell of buttery sandbakkel tarts and rolled krumkake. I figured I was trying to inhabit my mother's life, re-animate her. Why not? That seemed like a good place to start.

In the evenings, An taught me to draw. Later, as he slept, I arranged kelp bulbs and twisted pieces of driftwood on the kitchen table and tried to capture the bulk and weight of them. An and I had a good arrangement, nothing more, nothing less. I treasured being able to slide down beside him in bed at 3 a.m. and have him turn drowsily to say, "I have to check the kiln in an hour. What could we do between now and then?"

When he left each summer, I fed his tortoiseshell cat, and sketched the two square, cluttered rooms of our apartment 50 times. Then another 50. I graduated to moving objects and sat very quietly on the beach in my baseball cap, trying to catch the line of a volleyball player's arm or the twist of his shoulder. After a while, the regulars ignored me.

That September, An flew home to his family in Hong Kong for three weeks. He'd told me frankly that he was going to see a woman called Ling, whom he'd known since he was five years old. He came back alone, but we'd lived together for six years, and I could see that he'd changed. We bought him a cot for the far corner of the main room. One night, late, we sat on the cot in the dark. "I can't do this," I said. "I miss you too much." I turned to him. "No one would know."

He shook his head as he cried, his shoulders bent. From the side chair, the cat lifted his head as I rose and went to bed.

With this new arrangement, another year passed. I lied about my education and got a part-time position teaching adults beginning drawing Tuesday and Thursday evenings at the downtown rec center. By the time I turned 25, I was almost happy.

That October An flew home to his family in Hong Kong and married Ling. We arranged for me to keep the apartment. At four one morning, I wrote to him: "I now understand the phrase, 'I'm happy for you.' You saved my life. You deserve heaven on earth. Please send my warmest regards to Ling. She must have done something right to get you." I put down my pen that had a flat nib I sometimes used to give a sketch a filled line. Zeus lay down on my feet. During the day he was a hellion, but now he didn't even purr, as if that would disturb me. The only movement was his soft belly rhythmically pressing against my toes as he breathed. Now what?

Three days later, I came home to a message on the phone from my father. I had never given him my cell phone number. I only spoke to him every several years, usually on New Year's Day, when he called as if to take inventory of exactly where his genes were. Most days, I could barely imagine that he was my father.

The message said that he was dying. He was reduced to *this* to rope me back into his life! Rage rose so quickly I had to steady myself against the battered wood table that still smelled slightly of rotten sea things. My father's resonant voice that could hold 200 undergraduates in thrall had roughened a little. A faint rasp darkened the ends of some words. He said he had a proposition for me. He wanted to discuss it in person. Was there any way I could fly to Seattle this weekend?

Of course not. Was he crazy? I snapped the phone line off the jack, took the phone down the fire escape and tossed it in the heavy, scratched Dumpster. Damn him. Dying of *what*, pray tell?

He answered my cell phone on the tenth ring. "Dying of what?" I demanded.

"Emphysema."

"You don't smoke."

"It happens."

"What about a transplant?"

132

"Enlarged heart. Congestive. If I don't suffocate, I'll probably die of a big heart."

"Jesus. The irony."

Dryly, "Well said."

"Please don't comment on my comments. It's so post modern. So yesterday." I was scared, my voice high-pitched, silly. After all this time, I still sounded ridiculous when I talked to my father.

I hadn't set foot in Seattle for seven years. I stood on Capitol Way and looked up at my childhood home, which was on a slight, grassy rise with a hedge of gangly rhododendron. In the mornings, Santa Barbara air can be almost as misty as Seattle's, but light bounces through it from low, pink and yellow adobe buildings, from dew on front yards filled with ice plant, from the glistening sand that threatens to overtake any vacant spot. The air in Seattle, especially in the fall, is overloaded with the darkness of green things reaching for the sky. Thick grass along the walk to the porch seemed to spill chlorophyll into the almost-black leaves of the rhododendron against the heavy, black-streaked bark of our neighbor's cypress tree. The mist thickened above our stone chimney into freighted, unmoving clouds. The sun did not exist.

Yet I was almost faint with longing. My mother had discovered this house when she was a young bride, as she put it. Built in 1904, the house, with steeply pitched roof, was an abandoned derelict with floors so rotted that when she took my father to see it, a floorboard in the living room gave way under his foot. My mother replaced, sanded, and stained or repainted almost every surface in the house. It was her refuge and mine. It was the reason I believed that objects have a life worth drawing. Even when the brain goes dead with grief, the narrow back stairs lighted by three scalloped light fixtures live on.

Years before, when my father held court with his students in the galley kitchen, sitting on the linoleum counter, his feet on the seat of a chair while he argued and laughed with them, my mother and I climbed the stairs behind the kitchen to her "office" in the attic. She

133

paneled it in mahogany siding she found at a demolition sale in Fremont and furnished it with large, wicker chairs from the same sale. We called it our sun room.

Standing in the street, I could see the attic window next to the slate chimney. The only way to get to see it from the inside would be to knock on the door. Get past my father. Maybe pick him up and throw him off the porch. My nervous jokes made me more tense. I walked up to the front door that had a small inset of stained glass at eye level. I could see my father's rows of books in miniature, him. He opened the door.

He looked like someone had gone inside him and extracted about a third of his stuffing. His broad shoulders were racks of bone, and the folds around his eyes drooped to skin puddles in hollows beneath his pupils. The porch held the humid intimacy of a tent in the rain, but I stood back in confusion. I hated confusion. I hated him. Then why was I so glad to see that old plaid shirt of his and the big, slow smile? I imagined how I looked, my feet planted apart, the wavy hair I got from him blowing wildly in the gusts that slid down the trees like invisible waterfalls, the tensed lines of my eyes, my mother's blue eyes.

He glanced out to the curtain of rain sliding off the eaves, then back to me, the tiniest hesitation. My father hadn't been a man to hesitate. Finally he reached out his large hand and shook mine! I laughed nervously. "Okay." Not okay. His palm was papery, as if newly, delicately constructed.

We sat in the living room with five narrow windows. A fire blazed behind the black wrought-iron curls of the screen. My father didn't offer me food or drink, but launched right in. "The doctors say I have about a year," he said, "and I want you to live with me for that time and pretend to be my daughter."

"Nice. Sarcasm," I said. "Don't feel sorry for yourself. It's unbecoming."

He merely nodded, no retort. Since I'd seen him last, freckles had appeared at the top of his forehead, as if someone had sanded him down to a new layer. He touched the freckles with long

134

fingertips. "There would be no nursing, cooking, or cleaning. I have plenty of help. I'm rich, you know." He looked up.

"Me too," I said, realizing that sounded hysterical.

"I just want you to keep me company. And to be honest, to let my friends know that you didn't desert me completely."

My throat hurt. My feet, in wet sandals, ached as if I'd walked miles, though the cabbie had dropped me right at the curb. My father winced, as if a little tremor ran through his body. Wrinkles darted across his cheeks. Was he in pain? Wanting me to think he was in pain? I said, "You could have told them I was dead or in Argentina." Fatuous. I was becoming a 10-year-old.

My father gave a little shake of the head, as if shaking me off. Such a familiar gesture. He rarely wanted to be disturbed by what someone else said. He spoke, the cords of his neck shivering. "If you last the year, you get the house. Otherwise I'll give it to the U. Deal?"

The fire crackled and a log fell. "This house?" I couldn't hide my astonishment.

He shrugged with one shoulder and smiled. "You're the daughter. It's natural."

"I always thought it would go to the girlfriend of the hour. Whoever lands on the chair when the music stops, they get the prize."

"They teach you crudeness in Santa Barbara?"

"No, I taught myself, thank you." My mother's house. The lovely bead board under the chair rail in the dining room. The long rooms with high ceilings that I'd painted standing on the top step of a giant ladder. The leaded windows with wavy glass in diamond panes. My bedroom by the back of the house looking out on the pear tree. My young self returned to me. The attic.

I said, "Let me breathe for a minute." I crossed my legs. The broad arms of the flowered chair were clean, the room tidy, my father's magazines piled in the leather holder, the deep windowsills free of dust. My father was telling the truth about his help. "There must be a catch." I couldn't help myself.

"No catch. I've been de-fanged, as you can see."

My mother and I had spent a whole day hand-rubbing walnut stain into the wide planks of the floor at my feet. The next day we put on the lightest coat of urethane we could mix to keep it matte, not shiny. It still looked good, maybe a little darker. "One rule," I said. "You have to let me sketch your friends. I'll sit in the corner, and they'll forget about me."

He compressed his lips in a half-smile. "You're still drawing?"

I nodded, bracing myself.

"People?"

I nodded again.

"Narrative art. Didn't they tell you the center isn't holding?"

I hissed, "Unlike you, I believe that there's something outside myself that's interesting. What's more interesting than the figure? An infinite number of positions. I believe the line I make has something to do with the position of the figure, the person. At least *something*." My emphasis sounded defensive. I thought, Never defend, never apologize. That had been my rule with my father since I was a teenager. What had happened to me? I'd gotten soft. I thought of the gentle way An looked studiously to the side when I spoke, always waiting until I had finished my entire thought. Then asking me more about it.

My father snorted in amusement, started to speak.

"—second rule," I cut him off. "No criticisms. None. Nada."

The amusement shifted. He put his hand on his knee, a large, overturned bowl of bones. "I'll burst." The spreading smile.

"And no Jeanne."

The smile stopped. He lifted his palms. "Of course not."

I loved rules. An taught me three about drawing:

1. Draw what the figure is doing, not what he looks like. This pertains to all figures, especially models who are not moving.

2. Never draw your way out of trouble. Instead design your way out of trouble. This pertains to all subjects, especially those in nature. To understand this, look at Rembrandt's drawings.

3. Feet are notoriously hard to draw, unless you're Rembrandt. If you get in trouble with feet, lay a shadow across them. This will, strangely, anchor your figure.

136

I moved into my father's house; that is, my house. I tried to get one good, complete drawing of his helpers before he dismissed them. He fired the little, strong respiration therapist with the knot of hair at her nape because he couldn't stand the color of her nail polish (too orange).

At lunch one rainy day two months after I moved in, he barked at the cook/housekeeper with the jutting cheekbones that if he'd wanted a metallic taste in his chicken salad (she'd put in curry), he would have asked for it. He told her to go home and not come back. She glared at *me* and left.

My father, panting, went into the front room to wait for the new respiration therapist. I stayed in my mother's kitchen. I didn't want to talk to him. I had thought our agreement about criticism covered everyone in the house, but of course it didn't. I thought of the housekeeper's withering whisper to me as she gathered her bag: "I wouldn't let my *children* act like that." I was implicated—I'd accidentally touched my father's web. Our plates and glasses sat on the kitchen table all afternoon. The spoons in the glass seemed to scoop grayness. Rain scattered against the window over the sink at random intervals, as if someone were spraying a hose at us.

I missed the patch of weedy sand that led from my apartment (now subleased) to the beach. I missed An. I missed my dawn walk to work at the deli barefoot across the beach, my shoes in my hand.

I'd bought my mother's brand of dish soap, and its faint orange smell rose from the linoleum counter. The smell of despair. I sketched my father's coffee mug over and over. It became lumpy and bled into the darkening back of the chair. His unused spoon lay like a weapon at an angle. The slight wrinkle in the heavy tablecloth was a bunker.

My father stalked in. It was 3 p.m. but almost dark as night outside. He said, "You could at least pick up a dish."

"Not in my job description." A pause. "And I don't want to become my mother."

He sat in his chair with an elaborate sigh. I closed the notebook. He picked up the spoon, and I felt like he destroyed a landscape I was just figuring out. He glanced at the book and said, "You blame me for your lack of success."

I closed my eyes. "I don't want to split hairs with you over what constitutes a criticism." I *was* successful. Almost. If only I had my G.E.D., and someone to pour out my heart to besides my e-mails to An, and a venue to show my work besides one tiny gallery in downtown Santa Barbara and the dark wood walls of the deli. I felt myself sag, my shoulders tilting forward, my stomach caving—the posture of my youth. Damn him to hell.

He raised a brow and leaned back in the chair. I couldn't tell if he knew he hit the mark. Before his afternoon therapy, his face paled, and now his lips were mottled with gray. "I should have been a better father." He half-closed his eyes in self-pity.

I said fiercely, "Start now."

He looked at me. "I was hoping you would come to the living room to sit with me and chat. I waited for you."

"You don't *chat*."

He gave a little smile. "I was lonely. Am lonely."

"You just got rid of a perfectly good housekeeper. She was a great conversationalist."

A pause. He looked at me, and I wondered if he saw my mother's thin lips, her long neck. At last he said, "Did I tell you that my father taught me to read?"

I knew that his father, Anton, had lived in Olympia and been in charge of Special Collections at the main city library. My father's mother ran off with a state senator, and Anton died of a massive heart attack before I was born. My mother had remarked once that her father-in-law was a miserable human being who felt the world never appreciated him. He was tall, very thin, ate almost nothing (a sin in her book), and was as terse as my father was talkative.

Needing something to do with my hands, I got up to make coffee. My father couldn't drink his beloved Stoli shots anymore, but he still downed gallons of coffee, the one taste we shared. I wondered if his gloomy father drank coffee. I said, "You never talked much about Anton."

138

My father said quickly, as if he might run out of breath, "When I made too many mistakes on the words, he'd take a book in each hand and box my ears. I still have a ringing in them." A pause. A little smile. "Maybe that's why I was never good at listening."

His father hit him? The room stilled. I stopped pouring beans into the grinder. "How old were you?"

"Four."

Tenderness crept over me. I didn't want to be tender, but the words came out. "You must have been terrified."

He shrugged. "My father said that at the rate I was going, I was never going to live up to my potential."

"You were a little boy." I had thought that my survival depended on never forgiving. My mother's error had been to forgive too quickly. When she couldn't do that anymore, she didn't know how to live.

My father touched his chin with his first two fingers. They were bent a little at the last joint, a touch of arthritis. His chest had a very slight list to the right, as if the agony of trying to get enough oxygen had distorted him. He was slowly twisting down to earth.

I sat in my chair. The beans made a comforting racket as I touched the cuff of my father's shirt. "You never told me."

Again no hesitation, as if he had planned this. He nodded. "The awful thing is that I'm a lot like him." A breath through flared nostrils. "I'm drawn to weakness." A quick glance at me and then back at the table. "I can't help it. My students. A weak argument and I have to smash it. They called it brilliance." Another glance. "Fools."

I said softly, "You tried to destroy *me*."

Quickly, like a confession. "I was jealous of your youth."

"My mother had just died."

He pushed out several breaths. The therapist was late. My father could die right there with my hand reaching over to pat his cheek, to push away his tears. How did we get to this? He said in a whisper, "You could go on. I couldn't."

"I couldn't go on! I was scared." I rose and kissed the side of his bent head. The thick waves of his hair smelled dusty.

"You could. You did. Look what you've become."

139

For the next three months, I lived in the attic of our house, making the broad wicker sofa into my bed. My father's night nurse, a burly, retired paramedic, took my old bedroom. During the day, I sketched my father's friends and former students as they arrived in twos and threes for Saturday lunch or for dinner or just drinks by the fire. When I asked my father for more stories, he shrugged and said, "I've already played on your sympathies enough."

I made him coffee because the housekeepers could never get it right, and I brought him and his guests smoked salmon and capers with crackers I made like my mother because they had the right crispness with just the faintest chew in the middle. Occasionally my father caught my hand before I put down the square cushion on the corner bench by the last of the five living room windows. I'd smile at him and take out my working notebook to become a silent mouse in the corner.

My father's most frequent visitor was Travis Anderson, the statistician who had "done the numbers," as he said, for the famous Holmes study showing that even good events in one's life, like a happy wedding, create trauma so deep that one is more likely to, say, get in a car accident soon thereafter. In other words, if you're very happy or very sad, watch out. I was watching out. I was trying to believe in my father. I drew him as he sat wheezing by the fire with his old friend. One March night, their talk dwindled as wind blew like crashing waves through the cypress. My father's knees were splayed, his feet in socks flat on the wood floor. Without weight on them, his feet weren't very interesting. Yes, they were; I just couldn't get them right. The metatarsal jutted without relation to muscles or sinew. I couldn't reveal the architecture of the foot under the knit of the sock. Frustrated, I laid on shadow. It didn't do the anchoring it should. Oh, well. I moved over the page to Travis's long frame as he rubbed his knees and gazed into the fire. I drew the bend of his frame. Wrong. I laid a line next to the first. Almost. Again. Now, several Travises sat in the old, leather chair.

I looked at the man. Was he thinking about my father's coming death? Back to the drawing. In my hands, the bones of

140

Travis's face got longer and longer with each stroke, and his spine curved down unnaturally but with finality into the chair. I was not unhappy with the way the stray early lines made his figure possess the chair and not. If only I didn't have that damned, awkward shadow of my father in the other corner.

Travis got up. I couldn't remember if he and my father had been talking. Travis said, "Okay, I'll see you tomorrow."

My father nodded. Lately he'd been holding his chin out over his chest like a turtle. Sometimes at night, he coughed for long minutes, and I heard the night nurse cooing to him. He looked up. "It'll be fun," he said to his friend.

When Travis left, with a clattering of his umbrella and coat and mumbles of thanks to me (for what?), I came over to adjust the fire. Kneeling, I poked at the ash.

"What will be fun?" I asked my father.

There was a long pause. I thought he might be asleep. He'd laid his head off to the side on the pillow I'd propped up. Finally he said, "A little dinner party. Wendy is fixing everything." Wendy, the new cook hired on Sunday to replace the one my father said treated salt like an entrée. He rubbed his cheek along the pillow, an odd gesture of pain? of feeling the comfort of the cushion? of pleasure in just being with me? Hope rose. I didn't want hope.

"Are you all right?" I asked him. The wind had died to a pleasant rustle. A sense of near peace spread through me.

He wheezed, rolled his eyes. "Perfect."

I turned, smiled. The heat scorched my knees and the side of my face, but I didn't mind. I wanted this evening to last. "Travis is happy to be here."

Another smile. "*I'm* happy to be here."

That faint self-pity, but what did it matter? Tomorrow I'd try again to draw my father. For now I had the floorboards warmed by the fire under my bare feet, the folds of the linen curtains my mother and I had made, my father's unhurried willingness to just sit without reading or arguing. "Me too," I said.

141

I got up early the next morning, drove my father's Buick to the Pike Place Market, and bought bunches of iris, jonquils, and sunflowers (where in the world did sunflowers bloom in March?). I propped the flowers, wrapped in foil and newspaper, on chairs at my table on the third floor of Howell's Café by the big windows. I drank my small carafe of coffee called a hottle. Ferries majestically forged lanes across Elliott Bay. The sun crawled up over the fog bank and laid stars across the water. An's fourth rule was that if you don't start a drawing right, it'll never be right. I wasn't so sure. Maybe anything could be salvaged.

The new housekeeper, Wendy, who said she had eight children, all grown, toasted almonds for the halibut I'd gotten at the market, washed collard greens for sautéing, and made buttermilk biscuits. I was glad the meal would be little like what my mother would make. I arranged flowers and set them in large vases in the living room, dining room, and even kitchen. Working beside Wendy, I stirred together a mango salsa and also a hoisin sauce that An, an eclectic cook, had shown me. Wendy, pushing at the side of her very short, nappy hair, laughed and said that she'd resisted fusion until now. I plugged my iPod into my father's CD player and turned up the volume on some twangy country songs. Wendy, laughing, gave an exaggerated drawl, "You white folks sure do like some stupid rhymes." I grabbed her hand, and we danced in the little kitchen. Something was happening to me.

My father came out of the back bedroom. "I thought I told you," he deadpanned to Wendy, "no frivolity in my house."

She mirrored his stare and upped her Nashville drawl. "Believe me, Dr. Hintikka, this ain't no frivolity. This ain't hardly music."

He grinned. Unbelievable. Had I forgotten my father's non-ironic smile? A dimple appeared among the scattering wrinkles, and his eyes glistened. That smile, like Mount Rainier suddenly emerging, gleaming, from its bank of clouds. Anything was possible. I said to my father, "Watch out, or I might dance with you."

He took my arm and waltzed me in the little space between counter and chairs. He dipped his head with the beat like a little boy trying not to make a mistake in the rhythm. He reached up to let me twirl. Rhododendron blossoms waved outside the window. I bumped against Wendy's big behind. "I want hazard pay!" she cried.

The guests started arriving at seven. There were 19 of them, and they admired the flowers and talked about the weakened American dollar against the euro and told stories of their travels to Hanoi, Antarctica, and Santa Fe. I sat in my chair at the corner of the long table. Earlier Wendy had found silver candlesticks, cleaned off the tarnish with almost-dried polish she found in the back of the cupboard, and lit white candles. On the buffet she put five votives. "This isn't going to look séance-ey, is it?" I worried.

"No," she said without turning, "it's going to look Four Seasons-ey. We're going to make this poor old house glow!"

It did. The guests I remembered as acerbic and competitive settled into quiet chatter. Someone told an ancient golf joke, and everyone groaned good-naturedly. There was a knock at the door.

I jumped up, looking forward to seeing another person from my father's past, my past.

It was Jeanne. The street behind her had become a river of rain. She had aged into a tiny, brittle stick of a woman with flat black hair and lines shooting into her bright mouth. No. No!

That sly mouth. She said, "Oh, you're home. I didn't expect you home." She pulled back her tiny shoulders, gathering herself. "Is your father here?"

My heart shrunk to a spitball. "No," I said quietly. "He's not here." A pause. "My mother's not here either. But I'm sure you know that." I slammed the door.

I walked into the radiance of the dining room. Guests saw my face and stopped talking. I said loudly to my father, "Jeanne will not be joining us tonight. You will not get to watch me politely squirm. So sorry. That would have been fun. Your last hurrah. You win. I'm done." I turned to the women with big necklaces they'd bought for a song in desperate countries and the men who smelled of old wool and antacids. "He's all yours. Let's hope he didn't poison your dinner."

143

I walked through the kitchen and up the stairs. The fixtures were bloodless moons. I'd piled my sweaters and jeans on the glass table. I threw them in my duffel. I couldn't see. I fumbled for my cell phone in a jeans pocket, called Yellow Cab but got a steakhouse. I yelled at the waitress for a cab, dialed again.

My father, panting heavily, ducked under the slanting beams of the ceiling and stood with his chin cantilevered over his withered neck. "I didn't ask her to come. It was a coincidence." His breath rattled in his throat. The skin around his eyes quivered.

"Don't even," I said. "Just die. Get it over with."

"Honestly." He held onto the raw 4 X 4 in the middle of the tiny room. "I haven't seen her in years. Travis must have told her about the party."

I crushed a sweatshirt into a corner of the bag. I could send for the bigger things later—Wendy would pack them for me. "Shut up," I said quietly. "For once, just—"

"—I have everything to lose here. Why would I do that to you? To me? I love you."

I turned. "Right." My mind roared, yet a tiny doubt sneaked through. Jeanne *had* looked surprised. Was the coincidence possible?

My father sat heavily in the broad chair. "And you love me." His wheezing was wind in weeds.

I resisted his wheezing, the sheen of his face that could have been sweat, could have been tears. "I try not to," I said quietly.

"If you didn't, you wouldn't have such a big chip on your shoulder."

I sat on the rumpled quilt on the sofa, shook my head. Shook it again. My spirits slowed. The tip of the cypress was a dark shape outside the window. I knew my sharpness chased people away. Sometimes I lay in my bed in Santa Barbara and listened to the college kids on the street below laughing and sometimes whooping, and I'd think I was from another planet. I looked at my father. He blinked fast. He gasped for air. I was trapped in his meanness, mine. I was alone. The wind whispered through the shingles. I said, "You're right. But you get marked down for criticism."

144

He finally managed a big breath. "When I was ten—"

"—you were never ten." I would always be alone. "I don't care if your father beat you to a pulp. I can't live like this."

A second big breath. He was reviving from the long climb up the stairs. "He did beat me to a pulp. He had big hands like mine."

"I'm not listening."

"He used various excuses. The worst time, I'd spilled a drop of ginger ale on a copy of *Moby Dick* in his collection from the estate of the John Vancouver family. I was reading it when I wasn't supposed to. He pushed me into the bathroom and hit me so hard he broke my clavicle."

I squinted against the light spreading from the hanging lamp my mother had suspended from the low rafters. "Which page," I said, exhausted.

"Pip falls overboard. 'And Pip saw God's foot upon the treadle of the loom, and he spoke it, and therefore his shipmates called him mad.'"

The hard wicker back of the sofa against my neck was unyielding.

He said quietly, "I never hit you."

"So that was the standard?" Sarcasm was my instinct.

He shrugged and said sadly, "Maybe so."

I nodded absurdly. Someone rang the bell. My father and I both gave a start. The taxi. Or Jeanne trying again. We looked at each other. Three more rings. Then the sound of a car backing into the street and leaving. I didn't go to look. "Okay," I said. I would decide later what was okay and what wasn't.

I could hear the party breaking up below. The front door opening. More car engines being started. My father nodded. "Okay," he said. Maybe he was deciding too.

For three more months we lived in the same house and were civil to each other. My father got sicker. Most of the time he stayed in bed with oxygen hooked up. When I sometimes met him in the kitchen, his cheeks were dented from the tubing. When he sat down, I'd kiss him on the forehead. When Wendy had to take one of her grandkids

145

to the dentist or otherwise babysit, I poached his eggs and made him toast with orange marmalade, his favorite. Why not? He was my father. I couldn't figure out anything else.

One clear day in June, as Mount Rainier presided over the city, I went to the mailbox and found a letter to my father from the Development Office of the University of Washington. I didn't usually pry into his mail, but suspicion overwhelmed me, and I opened it. "Dear Dr. Hintikka: In appreciation for your generous gift, we would like to invite you to the..."

I ran up the three stairs of the porch and into the house. My father was slumped in his chair by the fire, a closed book on his lap, the book I'd fetched for him from the new library downtown. I held out the letter and said evenly, "You already gave away the house."

He looked up. Folds of skin tented his eyes. He gave a short sigh, almost a snort. "I did."

"All right," I said, turning. "The end. Finally."

He became very agitated. He put his palms to his temples. "How do you think I could afford all this care?" He looked at me, a twist of a twisted body. I towered over him.

He cried, "I couldn't go to a hospital! I couldn't live under the rules of some grandiose intern. You know I couldn't. It would have killed me."

"No jokes. We're past jokes. You gave away the house before I got here."

"I had to stay in the house. And I had to have you. This is my life. What's left of it. I love you."

"You're a monster."

"I love you. You have to believe that."

"I don't."

All was lost, so I could do whatever I wanted. What did I want? For some reason I stayed in the house. The nurse said my father wanted strawberries, so I got some at the market and cut them into tiny pieces so he could eat them. I covered them in cream the way he liked. I don't know why I did this. The nurse said he loved them.

146

Mornings I found the *Times*, usually under the cypress tree, and laid it on the kitchen table for him. I put a single lily in a vase for his tray. My mind was dead. I didn't know what I was doing.

He died two weeks later, about midnight. The nurse called the ambulance and then knocked on my door. I didn't go to see him. I'd seen enough of him. The nurse went with my father's body.

I wandered the house. I had the sensation that my mother had died again. I washed the kitchen counters. I put a fresh tablecloth on the long table. The cloth billowed and sank. I went into my father's room. The nurse had hung his coat on one side of the high-backed chair by the little bedroom desk. I stared at it for a long time. It was a thick wool with wide lapels. The black had softened to charcoal, and the lower hem brushed the floor.

The medical equipment stood in a corner on a metal table that must have belonged to the agency supplying the nurse. Should I call someone to get it? I couldn't move.

Finally my legs ached too much to stand. I climbed the stairs to bed. I immediately sank into sleep, waking just once. Everyone on earth had died. No. Just my father.

The next morning was bright. Foreign sun shocked my eyes. I found my notebook at the bottom of my duffel bag and went to Dad's room. I sketched his coat. Then I did it again. Again. The bend of the long collar and shaft of the arm held a little of the curve of his body. What was the coat doing? It was pulling to earth. I didn't need to do any more than that—just show the tension of gravity against the cloth's faint memory of my father. Just that. Again.

Every day I expected university officials to show up and kick me out, but they didn't. I drove my father's Buick to the market. I drank coffee. I bought bread and olive oil, sometimes a piece of salmon. I baked the fish in my father's ancient oven.

Then one day I took out my father's huge, wheeled suitcase, filled it with my clothes, the quilt, and my notebooks, boxed my mother's china with the wavy green edge, took the fireplace tools in case I ever had a fireplace, and drove my father's Buick back to Santa Barbara.

About a year after that, An wrote to say he wanted to visit with his wife and baby. I said, "Of course." I cooked for a week. I sent for delicacies. One night soon after I came to Santa Barbara, An had spread his hand on the sheet and said that some days he was a blind fish at the bottom of the ocean. I laid my hand on his and didn't move until he moved.

For his homecoming I asked local people if I could borrow the works of An's that they'd bought from him, and I set up a little gallery in the deli. The plates were on stands, the vases lined up on a shelf I'd cleared of liqueurs.

Ling wanted a tour of the apartment. She wore patent-leather shoes and a stylish linen suit. She had full, curved lips, a clear brow, and a slight Mandarin and French accent. An had said she was educated in Paris. She finished her English words with a lilt, a lingering tone, as if there could always be more to say.

She saw my drawings in the bedroom. "I like the cup series," she said.

They were done as my father drank coffee with me in the kitchen after he'd dismissed the housekeeper.

Ling turned to the wall by the window. "The people in chairs are complex. Not quite finished."

An came to the doorway with the baby, who had fuzzy hair standing straight up. For no reason, the baby laughed. An looked on and smiled at his wife and me.

"Ah," she said. "These are the ones to save." Ten attempts at my father's coat. "These show compassion," she said.

Sentimental, I thought, but didn't say. Lately I'd been waiting a little in conversations before cutting people off. Ling was just being nice to her husband's friend, but that counted. "You're bringing your own kindness to the picture," I said as I looked at my work. I'd almost forgotten that in the background I'd included faint suggestions of my father's bureau, the window he'd stared at, the cypress—an entire room. They were ghostly presences in opposition to the dominating coat.

148

Not listening, Ling kept looking at the sketches. "There's a fight going on. I can't explain. I'd like to take some of these back with me. I have friends at home in Hong Kong. They should see these."

They should? The sun dazzled the metal rim of my desk lamp. Joyous, southern sun. In my confusion I blurted, "I've finally learned that drawing is just graphite on paper."

She smiled. "Okay then." A pause.

An, my friend, holding his son, studied the last drawing in the row. He lifted the baby to his shoulder and looked at me. "Compassionate graphite," he said.

Tuesday and the Union
John J. Ronan

In Gloucester, on a street of bare oaks
And maples, the early sun's low,
Like five in July, except it's seven
On a November morning as the polls open

To public improvement of mood with coffee
And the boost of baked goods, a library
Benefit tempting our entire line,
Looped on itself a couple of times.

Neighbors in opposed passage say
"Hi" politely and with deference away
from easy chairs of what's what –
reverent weather, children, the Pats…

A worker asks for basic bio,
Name and address, and off you go
Behind the red, white and blue
Curtain of a brightly private booth

And in dark carbon make your marks,
Shedding self to become part
Of the anonymous, lifted will, pen
Trembling with the small movements of communion.

The stroll home's slow with sparrow
Feeding and hello in crucible cold,
Suffrage enough that quick witness,
The crumbs tumbling, yes, yes.

Crossings
Lara Gularte

All those years muddled
inside herself,
till her fear vanishes.

She lies suspended
in the dark
between wakefulness
and dream

where she begins
to understand
how near life
is to death,

how everything
sooner or later,
crosses over.

A prayer warms her mouth.
Birds fly across the sky
of her mirror.
Her shadow
wanders the room.

She used to think
her house had a ghost,
footsteps on the stairs,

the creaking door.
The ghost was her,
the imagined shadow
of herself.

In the morning,
what dream?
She endured the night.

She steps back
out of herself
and sees
where her footprints
turn
and walk the other direction.

reflections
Stephen W. Carter

I bring rules
that bind me
too tight

sight strained
by too strong
a desire to see

ripples on water
form no pattern
I can see

holding no single
wave I can ride

trees
deep-rooted
having withstood hurricanes
now stand
firm
on old roots

a few trees blown down
roots horizontal
exposed, still

live
send new trunks
straight up
compete with younger trees
for the scant sunlight

birds float
on water

far from here
the vines of a banyan tree
reach
toward earth
each to become
a trunk

one
of many

roots
trunks
past, present, future
still water
seemingly
flowing deeply
to the sea

memories refusing to rise
consciousness refusing to
sink into memory

all
is emptiness

reaching

warmup

maybe nothing.
maybe just an exercise.

but an exercise
as a warmup for a dance
is
or can become
the dance

we feel the body move
within the air
of a room

feel the body's push
against the resistance
of the floor
feel the body
sculpt out shapes
within the space defined
by walls, ceiling, floor.

exploration, discovery
of the body
through space.

though the exercise
may be repeated
"exactly as before"
every day,

the dancer hopes
that the room
has windows

that the light may fall
differently
each day.

Five Reasons for Forgetting to Tie Your Shoes
John Randolph Carter

The rump.
The main street wiggle.
The thump and fiddle of
the parlor butler.
The cat walk.

A considerable length of rope.
A rocky hillside littered with dead ideas.
A bowl in battle, carried by a gunnery sergeant.
A probable cause searching for a violent act.
A banana peel, unloved, unwanted.

An octopus and his point of view.
An outrageous fun zone filled with fatties.
An escalator on the mend.
An elephant sent home for Christmas.
An elevator operator without a license.

One solitary piece of neon candy.
Two bottles of beer on the wall.
Three trees with as many questions.
Four stars indicating the very best.
Five reasons for forgetting to tie your shoes.

Packrat
Robert J. Tillett

She calls things to her like gravity
Claims meteors, cosmic dust.
Basement loaded down with garage sale
Finds. Lamps, dinnerware, tchotchkes:
Little shepherds, angels, a well

With no bucket. No rope
On the windlass. No crank.
Tables of teapots, candy dishes,
Decanters from every holiday.
She'll go down to those rooms

To admire her trinkets, dust
The musty film from surface
And gap. Little arms reaching
For branches and other things high up.
Her one son studies stars and can see

That things accrete, heap, burn in flashes
On some distant star, rip matter
From nearby white dwarfs, other suns,
Dragging gas and substance through space,
Depletion in all its languages.

Her other son writes whatever he will,
Stories, poems—bits of porcelain chipped
From statuettes, from the marble bases
Of other children's trophies: spelling,
Golf, bowling. Other meditations.

Her children study space, words, silence,
Try to understand the basement, the hole
In their mother. The inevitable dust.
The falling behind. Buried alive
In the strata. Burning as fast as she can.

New Tattoo

God, forgive us this
ink. This four-letter smudge
on our knuckles. Forgive
us this doing, undoing—
this *HATE*, that *LOVE*.

Forgive us this ink.
This four-letter word.
That heart. Butterfly.
Dragon tails encircle our thighs,
scales where scales should be.

Forgive us this drunken
cross, that careless *Mom*
on bicep or forearm.
Blue-black, unsteady, thready
like our angry pulses.

Or sober and crisp, fiery skulls,
spiders, wisps of webbing on our elbows.
Anywhere the body bends,
contorts, a new image rises,
ends, a moon over rippling water.

Skin smudge, blue blot—
grandfathers home from war
for fifty years. Over coffee
in the corner shop, we wonder
what they were, these men,

those veiny crests, the fuzzy
oaths. Blurry answers to the old
questions. The code, the smeared
line, incomprehensible. Lodged
in the wrinkles. Nods as we pass.

My Devil
Will Tyler

Yours might wear satin, may be the smoking
man at the back of a room, seducer,

liar. Mine is much simpler
and more terrible. If God is word,

Satan's the white on the page, the space
language can't cover. The mad

scribbles we make, the reason
we spurn draft after draft,

for what is inspiration unrevised?
Perhaps Christian rappers might know.

It's the devil we blame for the torn canvas,
the smashed violin, the lines that never make it

into a poem. It's no wonder we think of him
as a lawyer in heavenly court, for what is a king

without exiles and those he's beheaded,
the questions cut down that only raise more?

It's Hell that aims us toward Heaven, offers
maps of its borders and pamphlets on how not to get in.

In the beginning there was the Word, and the Lord
in his wisdom crafted an editor, whom he hated

for all of the light that he brought, the questions
raised, but especially for the revisions

that the Lord knew were right and accepted
with great reluctance and a tearing of wings.

Wronged! No, Wrong Again
Laura Gamache

The hail unzips the sky with sound between
a moan and panic attack. My heart brattatats
as I scrawl notes. I'm not consoled nor lulled.

Where I come from we know that life's not fair
and no one will take care of us. But we
make thunder worse, serve curses piping hot.

I hate these days that pry the moldings off
the doors, tramp mud across the floors. And love
them too, spit threats like teeth. I whine my need,

a hatchet chopping round his heart, and this
another screed as floor falls out the fun-
house ride I'm spinning, clammy white, I crash

like branches through the light. It's not alright.
He lies beside me through the night. What are
we for? What do I always want but more?

To Her, in a Century We Can't Yet Speak of
Jonathan Greenhause

I'm trying to think *What would be the way to*
express herself on the white page, spill
her skin upon this swept surface? and
Who would she be? and *How to determine*
which "she" I'll write of? How futile
to specify and narrow the shower of flimsy adjectives.

She could be infinite. She could be
a goddess of everything intimate, a giver
to replace what's been stolen, a singer
of corporal praises. She could signal the end
to an era of abandonment. She could be
nothing, just imagination,
a variety of velleities. A treasure of
trivialities. An anarchy of eventualities.

Her pleasing vision could lead
to a bevy of epiphanies, a litany
of laudatory verses verging on
idolatry. Her mission would accompany
a mass of amorous accolades, or maybe
she's supremely plain and principally
not much to speak of. Maybe
she's her, the shy one staring at the reflection
of a *Sale* sign in the window, her fingers tracing
the exact amount of this weekend's discount.

Maybe she's sitting on her bed, writing
a trashy romance novel. Maybe she's just
shattered a molar with a hard pretzel. Maybe
she's myself in a dress and long black stockings.
Maybe she doesn't speak English. How can I be
so convincingly assured to even think
she'll read this? Maybe she's waiting for me
two centuries in the future, and she's
reading these lines and sighing. Or maybe
she'll be relieved to never meet me.

what I should have done
David Spiering

I should have written
as if it were the last week
on earth; but I wrote
from my usual outsider
perspective
observing how life
happens in front
of me as well
as what is in the dark
peripheries—I'm
alone with my wish
that someday
while standing next
to a frozen lake
I'll look up
at the stars
in the winter
to see a path
that leads
me to joy

Contributors

Kristin Berkey-Abbott earned a Ph.D. in British Literature and has published in many journals. Pudding House Publications published her chapbook, *Whistling Past the Graveyard*. Currently, she teaches and serves as Chair of the General Education department at the Art Institute of Ft. Lauderdale. Her website, with her blog links, is www.kristinberkey-abbott.com.

Jodi Adamson is a retail pharmacist with a Pharm D. In her spare time, she dabbles in creative writing. Her poetry has been published in *The Griffin*, *The Old Red Kimono*, *The Prelude*, and *RiverSedge*. *The Ten Commandments for Pharmacists*, written by her and illustrated by Stacey Hopson, is a humorous, illustrated book about the world of pharmacy and is available on the Xlibris website.

Rachel de Baere teaches ongoing writing practice groups in the San Francisco Bay Area and offers writing retreats, editing, and project coaching throughout the United States and Europe. In 2009, Rachel's work appeared in the *Hurricane Review*, *RiversEdge*, *Limestone*, *Poetry Flash*, *Oregon East*, and *Darkling*. A member of the International Women's Writing Guild Board of Directors and faculty, Rachel is also a member of the *Poet's Roundtable, the California State Poetry Society, the Marin Poetry Center, Left Coast Writers* and the 2010 faculty of the *Afghan Women's Writing Project*. Her current writing projects are a memoir and a poetry manuscript.

Laurie Blauner is the author of six books of poetry and two novels. Her most recent book of poetry is *Wrong*, from Cherry Grove Collections. Both of her novels are from Black Heron Press. Her poetry and fiction have appeared in *The New Republic*, *The Nation*, *The Georgia Review*, *The Seattle Review*, *The New Orleans Review*, *Poetry*, and *American Poetry Review* among others. She lives in Seattle, Washington.

Randy Blythe teaches and writes at the University of Alabama at Birmingham. His poetry has appeared in a variety of publications, among them *Southern Humanities Review, Poet Lore, Laurel Review, Tar River Poetry, Black Warrior Review, Northwest Review, South Carolina Review,* and *Spoon River Poetry Review.*

Renee Taylor Boeckman grew up in the Pacific NW, where many galleries provided awe and inspiration during family visits. Her work is best described as a combination of impressionism and representational art. "Before the bronze made these faces solid, permanent images of the past, clay was pulled and carved and pieces were merged with refreshing calmness. Time spent in isolation reminds me that we hold many faces throughout our lives—more than we can recall. We not only hold our own masks and faces of change, but images of people from the past, recalling beliefs and influences. We do not live in isolation as we are pulled, carved, and merged with the images of our memories in the 'Faces I Remember.'" 2000, 12"x10." Photo by Randy Taylor.

Wanda Lea Brayton was born in Kansas, raised in Oklahoma, and is presently residing in Nebraska. She is a former college librarian and construction news reporter, and has been a poet since 1973. She has approximately 90 poems listed in various anthologies, and her first solo book of poetry was released in May 2006. She is currently gathering material for a second book. She is influenced by Dickinson, Millay, Neruda, and many others. Her favorite obsessions include reading, writing, watching movies, listening to music, walking in parks, and eating ice cream, all in the company of her brilliant husband, who is also a writer. Her poetry can be found by searching for "Night Hope" at www.allpoetry.com.

Traci Brimhall is the author of *Rookery,* winner of the 2009 Crab Orchard Series in Poetry First Book Award. Her poems have appeared in *New England Review, Virginia Quarterly Review, Kenyon Review Online, The Missouri Review, The Southern Review,* and elsewhere. She has also received the Jay C. and Ruth Halls Poetry Fellowship from the

171

Wisconsin Institute for Creative Writing and a Tennessee Williams Scholarship from the Sewanee Writers' Conference.

Bryan C. Brunton was born and raised in Kansas and lives and works in Colorado. In late 2009, he was so intensely disappointed at missing a friend's poetry reading that during the drive of some five hundred miles home he began composing a poem. The ensuing merriment proved to be more than road fatigue induced delirium, and he hasn't stopped since.

Ben E. Campbell is a native of West Virginia's Alleghany Highlands. He and his beautiful wife continue to reside in the Southern Appalachians, currently calling Giles county, Virginia, their home. Other fictional works of his are in *The Roanoke Review* and the anthology *The Artist as Activist in Appalachia*.

Carol Carpenter's poems and stories have appeared in *Margie*, *Snake Nation Review*, *Neon*, *Georgetown Review*, *Caveat Lector*, *Orbis*, and various anthologies. Her work has been exhibited by art galleries and produced as podcasts (*Connecticut Review* and *Bound Off*). She received the Hart Crane Memorial Award, the Jean Siegel Pearson Poetry Award, and other awards. Formerly a college writing instructor, journalist, and trainer, she now devotes her time to writing in Livonia, MI.

John Randolph Carter is a poet and artist. A finalist for the *National Poetry Series*, his poetry has appeared in journals including *Bomb*, *The Cream City Review*, *LIT*, *Margie*, *North American Review* and *Verse*. He has been the recipient of N.E.A., New York State Council, and Fulbright grants. His art is in thirty-two public collections, including the *Metropolitan Museum of Art*. One-person exhibitions include *The University of Michigan Art Museum* and the *Minneapolis Institute*.

Stephen W. Carter taught music and English at Berklee College of Music for many years. He now works as a professional jazz guitarist and as a software engineer, while continuing to write poetry, fiction, and non-fiction. His poetry has appeared in *Carolina Quarterly, Wisconsin Review, Hiram Poetry Review, Pacific Review, Orphic Lute, Hanging Loose,* and other magazines. His non-fiction has appeared in *Guitar Player, db - The Sound Engineering Magazine, Drums and Drumming,* and other magazines.

Renee Emerson lives in Louisville, KY, with her husband. She has her M.F.A. in poetry from Boston University and was the recipient of the Academy of American Poets prize from Boston University. Her work has appeared in *Tar River Poetry, The Blue Earth Review, Existere, Third Wednesday, The American Literary Review, Grasslimb Journal, Sage Trail,* and *Plain Spoke,* among others. Her first chapbook, *Something Like Flight* is available at www.sargentpress.webs.com.

Judson Evans is Director of Liberal Arts at The Boston Conservatory. His work has been published in *Volt* and in *New Smoke: An Anthology of Poems Inspired by Neo Rauch.* He was chosen as an "emerging poet" for the Association of American Poets, by John Yau, in Sept. of 2007.

Rebecca Foust's book *All That Gorgeous, Pitiless Song* won the Many Mountains Moving Book Prize and was released in 2010. Also released in 2010 was *God, Seed,* a collection of environmental poetry with art by Lorna Stevens. Two chapbooks, *Mom's Canoe* and *Dark Card,* won the Robert Phillips Poetry Chapbook Prizes in 2007 and 2008.

Seattle poet and educator **Laura Gamache** has published on radio, buses, tee shirts, bookmarks, online in *LocusPoint: Seattle* and *Avatar Review,* and in anthologies. Her work has appeared or will appear in journals including *Crab Creek Review, Pontoon, Vol. 7* and *10* and *The South Dakota Review.* Finishing Line Press published her chapbook, *nothing to hold onto,* in 2005.

Jonathan Greenhause works as a Spanish interpreter, is the proud papa of a leopard-spotted African frog, and spends a large chunk of each day admiring his fiancée's stand-up comic skills. His poetry has appeared or is forthcoming in over a hundred literary reviews, most recently in *The Chaffin Journal, Interim, Quiddity, Slab, Slipstream,* and *Thin Air.*

Robert H. Guard attended Ohio University where he studied poetry writing under Wayne Dodd and Bin Ramke. After graduation, he became an advertising copywriter and has worked in the marketing field for most of his career. He completed the Kenyon Review Writers Workshop for a second time was invited back to attend future workshops. The common denominator in his poetry is a fascination with the spiritual realm. His poems have appeared or are forthcoming in *Argestes, The Chaffin Journal, descant, Eclipse, Nimrod, Quercus Review, Sycamore Review,* and *Harpur Palate.*

Lara Gularte earned an M.F.A. from San Jose State University where she received several Phelan Awards and the Anne Lillis Award for Creative Writing. Her poetry has appeared in such journals as *California Quarterly, Hiram Poetry Review, Evansville Review, Bitter Oleander, The Fourth River, Monserrat Review, Water-Stone Review,* and *Watershed,* and has been translated into Portuguese by the University of the Azores. In July of 2008, she was a resident poet at the Footpaths to Creativity Writer's Residency and Retreat on Flores Island in the Azores. She is an assistant poetry editor for *Narrative Magazine.*

Pamela Gullard's stories have appeared in the *North American Review, Arts and Letters, The Iowa Review, TriQuarterly,* and other journals and anthologies. Her collection, *Breathe at Every Other Stroke,* published by Henry Holt, includes a story that won a PEN Syndicated Fiction Project Award, and another that was nominated for a Pushcart Prize. In 2009, Scottwall Associates published her third nonfiction book, written with Nancy Lund, *Under the Oaks: Two Hundred Years in*

Atherton. Pamela lives in Menlo Park with her husband Mike and their two sons.

Kathleen Haley has published poems in the *Oregonian* and the *Journal of Medical Humanities*. She has studied with Judith Barrington, Naomi Shihab-Nye, and Ana Callan. She currently lives in East Portland, Oregon, with a view to the beautiful open reservoirs of Mt. Tabor.

Daniel Harrington supports his writing habitat with jobs in wildlife biology throughout the West. He has currently landed in Washington, on the east slopes of the North Cascades. He has non-fiction published in *Oregon Literary Review,* is a former editor of *Oregon East,* and had the pleasure of seeing one of his poems displayed on the Juneau bus system for a year. He authors a blog at http://danielharrington.wordpress.com.

Kelly I. Hitchcock is a novelist, poet, and blogger from a poor stretch of the Ozarks in Southwest Missouri. A graduate of the creative writing program at Missouri State University, Kelly loves music, writing about music, learning about and using new technology, designing and making her own clothes, and playing amateur dodgeball. She lives in Kansas City and is an avid volunteer and fundraiser for the Cystic Fibrosis Foundation. Learn more about the author and her work at www.KellyHitchcock.com.

Karen Holmberg's poems have appeared or are forthcoming in such magazines as *Southern Poetry Review, Hotel Amerka, West Branch, Subtropics,* and *New Madrid*. She teaches in the MFA program at Oregon State University.

Christopher Howell, an Oregon native, most recently published *Light's Ladder* and *Dreamless and Possible: Poems New and Selected* (University of Washington Press), and *Gaze* (Milkweed Editions). He has received three Pushcart Prizes, two fellowships from the National Endowment for the Arts, and fellowships from the Washington Artist Trust and the Oregon Arts Commission. He has also been awarded

175

the Washington State Governor's Prize, the Washington State Book Award, and the Stanley W. Lindberg Award for Editorial Excellence. He teaches at Eastern Washington University's Inland NW Center for Writers, in Spokane.

Lori Kagan grew up in Northbrook, Illinois, and currently lives near Boston, Massachusetts. She has a degree in journalism from the University of Kansas. Her work has appeared or is forthcoming in literary journals including *Oregon East, Lullwater Review, Eureka Literary Magazine, North Atlantic Review, Sulphur River Literary Review, Slipstream, Evansville Review, South Carolina Review,* and *Studio One.* Her poem "I Dip My Skirt in Your Blood John Dillinger" was nominated for a Pushcart Prize: Best of the Small Presses.

Noel Kalenian is from Grand Junction, Colorado, a high desert town. He has lived in New York City and San Francisco (where he received his MFA in Creative Writing), and currently lives in Denver. He has had fiction and poetry published in *Fourteen Hills, New Millennium Writings, Sidebrow, South Dakota Review,* and *Thin Air Magazine.* He is at work on a novel and a manuscript of poems.

Robert King's work has recently appeared in *Rattle* and *Louisiana Review.* His first book, *Old Man Laughing,* was a finalist for the 2008 Colorado Book Award in Poetry. He lives in Greeley, Colorado, where he directs the Colorado Poets Center.

W.K. Lawrence has published poems and fiction in various national and international journals. He is the author of several poetry chapbooks and one book. He lives in Virginia and teaches English at George Mason University. He is currently working on various projects, which include academic writing and a memoir.

D. Lifland is a writer on the East Coast. During college, he wrote poetry, short fiction, and plays, but for the past decade, he has focused solely on poetry. He has poems that have or will be published in literary magazines across the country. As an artist, he greatly admires John Coltrane, Stanley Kubrick, and Antoni Gaudí.

Christina Lloyd completed a master's degree in creative writing from Lancaster University, U.K., in the fall of 2008. Her work appears in *Monday Night, Fawlt Magazine, Rio Grande Review, Pearl Magazine, Colere,* and *Red Rock Review.* She currently teaches Spanish and lives by the ocean in San Francisco.

Jerome Long is a retired writer/editor who has worked in the communications departments of several not-for-profit scientific and educational institutions in the Chicago area. After retirement, he took up writing poetry and fiction, long-postponed ambitions, because he wanted to write what he felt and wanted to say, not what others directed him to write.

Raymond Luczak is the author and editor of more than ten books, including *Mute: Poems, Men with Their Hands: A Novel,* and *Assembly Required: Notes from a Deaf Gay Life.* A filmmaker and playwright, he lives in Minneapolis, Minnesota. Learn more about the author and his work at www.raymondluczak.com.

Stephen Massimilla's books and poems have won various awards, including the Sonia Raiziss-Giop Bordighera Book Prize, the Grolier Poetry Prize, a Van Renssalaer Award, an Academy of American Poets Prize and two Pushcart nominations. He has new work in *Agni Review, Barrow Street, Chelsea, The Colorado Review, The Denver Quarterly, The Greensboro Review, Natural Bridge, Paterson Literary Review, Provincetown Arts, Quarterly West, Verse Daily,* and elsewhere. He received an MFA and a Ph.D. from Columbia University, where he teaches classics and modernist literature.

Lloyd Milburn earned an MA in English with a creative writing thesis. He has been teaching composition and creative writing for over fifteen years. He is currently nearing completion of his first book of poetry. His lifelong love for music and an interest in science inform his writing.

Ann Minoff graduated from New York University with a degree in philosophy and continued her education at the National College of Chiropractic in Illinois. She received her Doctorate of Chiropractic in 1982. She currently teaches Qigong and classes on Kabbalah. Her work is forthcoming or has been published in *The Alembic, The Distillery, The Literary Review, Lullwater Review, Nimrod, Porcupine, Quiddity Literary Journal,* and *Sacred Journey: Journal of Fellowship in Prayer.*

Linda Lancione Moyer writes poetry, essays, and fiction. Her work has appeared in *Atlanta Review, Cimarron Review, CrazyHorse, Jabberwock, The MacGuffin, Notre Dame Review,* and *Post Road,* among other literary journals, and will soon appear in *Compass Rose, Connecticut Review,* and *Eclipse.* Her most recent chapbook, *2% Organic, 32 Short Poems from a West Marin Dairy Barn,* is a best seller at Mrs. Dalloway's in Berkeley, California, her local independent bookstore. She's recently been a resident at the Helene Wurlitzer Foundation in New Mexico.

Over a hundred of **James B. Nicola**'s poems have appeared (or are about to) in publications including *The Texas Review, The Lyric, Nimrod, Upstart Crow, Mobius,* the *Alabama Literary Review,* and *Cider Press Review.* He also won the Dana Literary Award for poetry and received a Rhysling Award nomination. A stage director by profession, his book *Playing the Audience* won a CHOICE Award. Also a composer, lyricist, and playwright, his musical *Chimes: A Christmas Vaudeville* premiered in Fairbanks, Alaska, with Santa Claus in attendance on opening night.

Darlene Pagán teaches literature and writing at Pacific University in Forest Grove, OR. Her poetry is forthcoming or has most recently appeared in *Hiram Poetry Review, Hawaii Pacific Review, While Pelican Review, Two Review: An International Journal of Poetry and Creative Nonfiction, The New Verse News,* and *Willow Springs.* Her essays have appeared in *The Nebraska Review* and *Literal Latté.* Her current passions are playing The Flash to her toddler sons' Batman and Robin and looking for worms in the rain.

Raegen Pietrucha received her M.F.A. from Bowling Green State University, where she served on the staff of *Mid-American Review*. Her work has been published in *Cimarron Review, Puerto del Sol, Edge, The Northridge Review*, and other magazines.

Jenny L. Rife lives with her husband and family in northern Kentucky, where she is pursuing a degree in English from Thomas More College. She also writes fiction, and is currently at work on a novel. This is her first publication.

Matthew Campbell Roberts is an English instructor and lives in a cabin near the Skokomish and Union Rivers. His latest work appears in *StringTown*.

Justin Rogers pays his way by performing as a night watchman. *Off the Coast, EDGZ, POETALK, Poiesis, First Class*, and *Barbaric Yawp* have recently published his poetry.

John J. Ronan is a poet, playwright, and movie producer. He was named a National Endowment for the Arts Fellow for 1999-2000, and in 2008, he was appointed Poet Laureate for Gloucester, MA. Ronan's most recent book of poetry is *Marrowbone Lane*. His comedy, *The Yeats Game*, ran at the Boston Playwrights' Theatre in 2008, and his comedy, *10,000 Years Later: A Parable in Two Acts,* was produced in 2010. He is also the founder of American Storyboard, a documentary production company.

Joanna Rose is the author of the award-winning novel *Little Miss Strange*, and has recently completed a second novel. Her essay "Paisley Afternoon" is in the anthology *Citadel of the Spirit*, and other work has appeared in *ZYZZYVA, Four and Twenty, High Desert Journal, Bellingham Review, Story Magazine*, and *Northern Lights*. She is also known to readers of *The Oregonian* as a regular book reviewer. She and her teaching partner Stevan Allred host the Pinewood Table critique group, and she works with writers of all ages in schools around Portland, Clark County, and the beach. Especially at the beach.

Amy Schutzer is an award-winning poet and fiction writer who lives in Portland, Oregon. Her first novel, *Undertow*, was a Lambda Book Award finalist, Violet Quill Award finalist, and Today's Librarian Best of 2000 Award winner. Her poetry has appeared in a variety of literary reviews and magazines including *Portland Review*, *Fireweed*, *HLFQ*, *Sequoia*, and *Hurricane Alice*. She is the recipient of an Astraea Foundation Grant for Fiction (1997) and a grant from the Barbara Deming Memorial Fund (1999). While publishing her 2nd and 3rd novel remain on the horizon, she is hard at work on a fourth novel, and always, poems.

Judson Simmons is a graduate of the Sarah Lawrence College Writing Program and holds a BA in writing from the University of Houston. He currently works at the University of Houston as a Program Coordinator for the College Success Program. His chapbook, *The Hallelujah Hour*, is available from Amsterdam Press. His poems have appeared in *Evergreen Review, Folio, Pebble Lake Review*, plus other journals.

David Spiering's first full-length poetry collection, *My Father's Gloves*, is available from Sol Books Minneapolis. Editors tell him the *Midwest Book Review* has reviewed his book. Jobs he has done to support himself while he writes: co-op baker, natural foods and produce clerk, cook, and college professor.

Christine Hope Starr holds an MFA from Vermont College of Fine Arts, which nominated her for Best New Poets 2009. Her work appears or is forthcoming in *California Quarterly, Cider Press Review, Eclipse, Front Range Review, Manorborn, Permafrost*, and *Spoon River Poetry Review*. She dances after dinner with two daughters who know all the new moves.

Oklahoman by birth, Arizonan by circumstances, **Dorothy Stroud** taught language arts for nineteen years in public school, while accumulating a family and other experiences, including drying laundry outside in Alaska in the wintertime and crying on a visit to the Holocaust Museum in Washington D.C. Her current involvement is co-grandparenting while she searches for people to read her poetry.

Robert J. Tillett holds MA and MFA degrees in creative writing and poetry from SUNY Brockport and the University of Arkansas, Fayetteville, respectively. He was a winner of a Breadloaf Writers' Conference Scholarship, and his poetry has been twice nominated for a Pushcart. His work has appeared in David Wagoner's *Poetry Northwest*, *Borderlands: Texas Poetry Review*, *Red Wheelbarrow*, *Southern Indiana Review*, *Coe Review*, *ABZ*, *Harpur Palate*, *River Oak Review*, and *Sugar House Review*.

Will Tyler currently lives in Jackson, Tennessee, with his wife and son. He works from home as a freelance proofreader and copy editor but spends much of his day chasing after his energetic child. His poems have also appeared in *The Los Angeles Review*, *Crab Orchard Review*, and *Albatross*.

James Valvis lives with his wife and their daughter in Issaquah, Washington. His poems have appeared in *5 AM*, *Confrontation*, *Green Hills Literary Lantern*, *Hurricane Review*, *New Laurel Review*, *New York Quarterly*, *Nimrod*, *Pearl*, *Rattle*, *Slipstream*, *Southern Indiana Review*, and others.

Paul Weidknecht's work has appeared in *The Los Angeles Review*, *The Vocabula Review*, *Yale Anglers' Journal*, *The Oklahoma Review*, *Sunken Lines*, *Hitotoki* (New York), *Outdoor Life*, *Potomac Review* online, and elsewhere. He has written a feature-length screenplay, *A Storm in Season*, about a former slave who became the first African-American war hero, and is currently at work on a novel. He lives in northwest New Jersey.

Lindsay Wilson teaches college in Reno, Nevada, where he also edits the literary magazine, *the Meadow*. He has authored four chapbooks, been named a finalist for the Philip Levine Prize, and has poetry published *The Portland Review*, *Salamander*, *The South Dakota Review*, *Gulf Stream*, and *The Blue Mesa Review*, among others.

Visit

on the web at

clackamasliteraryreview.org

facebook.com/clackamasliteraryreview

Contact

CLR
CLACKAMAS LITERARY REVIEW

at

clr@clackamas.edu

CLACKAMAS LITERARY REVIEW

the finest writing for the best readers

Clackamas Literary Review has been committed to bringing you the
best writing from around the world since 1997.
Subscribe now to receive the latest and forthcoming issues.

Clackamas Literary Review

_____	1 year	$10
_____	2 years	$18
_____	3 years	$26
Name		
Address		
City/State/Zip		
Email		

Send this form and check or money order to:

Clackamas Literary Review
Clackamas Community College
19600 Molalla Avenue
Oregon City, Oregon 97045